A Candlelight Ecstasy Romance™

FOR A MOMENT,
SHE RESISTED. . . .

Then she went limp against him, reminding herself that this would be all she would have of Quentin. He would send her away today, she was sure.

"Quent," she pleaded, kissing him as she had never kissed him before, feeling his heart thunder against her. Reveling in the knowledge that she had the power to arouse him as he was arousing her, she sighed and lifted her fingers to unbutton his shirt.

He pulled back, his strong mouth shaking, his face white under the dark tan. "No, Chara."

"Why?" She pouted, feeling reckless.

"Because we're getting married in less than an hour."

TO LOVE
A STRANGER

Hayton Monteith

A CANDLELIGHT ECSTASY ROMANCE™

Published by
Dell Publishing Co., Inc.
1 Dag Hammarskjold Plaza
New York, New York 10017

ISBN: 0-440-14798-0

Printed in the United States of America
First printing—June 1982

Dear Reader:

In response to your continued enthusiasm for Candlelight Ecstasy Romances™, we are increasing the number of new titles from four to six per month.

We are delighted to present sensuous novels set in America, depicting modern American men and women as they confront the provocative problems of modern relationships.

Throughout the history of the Candlelight line, Dell has tried to maintain a high standard of excellence, to give you the finest in reading enjoyment. That is now and will remain our most ardent ambition.

Anne Gisonny
Editor
Candlelight Romances

*To my husband—the most romantic man
in the world, who is my friend,
my support, and my love*

TO LOVE
A STRANGER

CHAPTER ONE

Chara Styles could feel her long pale-pink fingernails digging into her palms as she watched her mother approach with a black-haired Hercules beside her. How like her mother to have a movie idol in tow, Chara thought. *Lord, I'm getting waspish.* Even though Chara didn't recognize him, she was sure he would be famous. Her mother always sought that type of man. When her father was alive, he also preferred the company of the "beautiful people." Chara had always known that she and her brother Ken hadn't figured highly on their parents' list of priorities. She wished now that she hadn't given in to Ken's pleas to accompany him to their mother's desert home. She knew he needed her support, but Chara made it a practice to avoid her mother whenever possible. She was content to pursue her own career as a paralegal for the county of Los Angeles. She felt Ken stiffen at her side as their mother called to him. She couldn't know that her brother's taut look was reflected in herself. She took a deep breath.

"Please, Chara, don't let her goad you into saying anything that would tip the scales against me," Ken whispered. "You know how she loves to needle you, and how quickly you rise to the bait. I want this job, Chara. I want to get into movie work. I know you don't care for this type of work, but I do."

"Well, someone in the family was bound to be sane enough to stay out of this crazy business," Chara hissed.

"Chara, you promised. Be good. I need you to stand by me." Ken gulped, touching her arm.

"All right, all right, Ken." Chara soothed her brother. "I am standing by you." She leaned closer to her brother. "I just hope this won't be another one of those charades where she points out to anyone who will listen how amazing it is that she can have such uninspired children when she herself is so talented."

Before Ken could do more than swallow a guffaw, their mother was with them, the ever-present cigarette holder jabbing the air like a spear, her gold hair glistening in the hot desert sun. "Q, darling, this is Kenwood Foster Styles, Jr. My son." Her bored glance swung to her daughter. "This is Chara Lincoln Styles, my daughter." Her look turned to a beaming smile as she gazed at the man next to her. "Kenny, Chara, this is Quentin Wainwright, the director. You may recall that he produced and directed *Adelaide* and *Spendthrift.* Both, of course, were incredibly successful," Meta Lincoln Styles stated with a satisfied air as she clasped Quentin's arm possessively. "Q and I work so well together." A light frown barely creased the perfectly made-up face as she looked back at her children. "It's Kenny who wants a job. Chara isn't interested in our work. She does . . . something in an office, I think. Secretary, perhaps. She has shown no aptitude for writing. Amazing, isn't it, considering that I'm her mother. Their father was a writer too, Quent. Fos was a bastard, but he had talent." Meta shrugged, exhaling a stream of smoke through her nose.

Angry, Chara shook off her brother's restraining hand. "That's not exactly accurate, Mother." Chara said sweetly. "I wanted to co-author *Mommie Dearest* with Joan Crawford's daughter, but I lost out."

Ken's anguished "Chara, please" and her mother's angry gasp were drowned out by Quentin Wainwright's shout of laughter.

Chara bit her lip and turned to look at the amused director. *I'll bet they work well together,* she thought, *Adonis and the Queen Bee.* She became aware that he was watching her as closely as she was watching him. It infuriated her to find those liquid silver eyes raking her from head to toe, as though he were removing her clothing one article at a time.

When he shook her hand, she stared at a point just past his right ear. She inhaled a breath when she felt his index finger stroke her palm in a deeply sensuous caress. She tried to yank her hand free of him, but his grip wouldn't release her. "Mr. Wainwright," Chara grated, "I am not the one interested in a job. Kenny is—"

"Really, Chara, you needn't interfere. I will ask Q about a job for Kenny," her mother interrupted. "Perhaps your secretarial course didn't teach you about manners . . ."

"Paralegal, Mother. I'm a paralegal for the county of Los Angeles. We assist lawyers in preparing their briefs and related law work." Chara let her gaze touch Quentin Wainwright. "I'm talking about the real world, Mother. I prefer it to waltzing through Alice's looking glass."

"Meaning my world, I suppose?" Quentin Wainwright drawled, laughing down at her, keeping her hand in his. "Pompous, aren't you." Again his index finger etched across the palm of her hand, sending tremors down her spine.

Fuming, Chara's eyes locked with his amused ones.

"How do you do, Chara." The voice abraded Chara's nerves. "It's very nice meeting you." His grin widened as

13

she pulled at her hand again. "Be nice and I'll release you," he whispered.

"How do you do, *Mr. Wainwright*," Chara spat out as he let go so suddenly that she staggered.

"Q? What are you saying to Chara? Did you hear what I said?" Meta rasped, her smoke-roughened voice irritated. "Kenny wants a job in the business. He majored in theater arts at UCLA. I said I'd ask if you had a spot for him." Meta shrugged, taking a long drag on her almost-foot-long smoking gear. To Chara it sounded as though her mother would understand if Quentin turned Kenny down.

"Umm? What did you say, Link? A job for Ken? Maybe." He assented, still not looking away from Chara.

Startled at the answer, Chara's eyes widened on the director. She felt caught in his stare like a fly in a web. For the first time in many a year, she could feel a blush coating her skin. *Damn him, why doesn't he look elsewhere?* She pushed a trembling hand through her hair. When she turned away from him to look at her mother, she felt a giggle start in her throat. Meta was staring at Quentin, mouth agape, the cigarette holder pointing to the ground. Ken's delighted surprise had riveted him to the terrazzo. The only one of the foursome who seemed to be relaxed was Quentin himself.

"Do you mean it?" Ken husked.

"I always mean what I say. Here, take this card; present it at Reception." He seemed indifferent to the other two as Ken grasped the embossed card. Quentin's eyes were still devouring Chara, making her feel angry and uncomfortable.

Without saying another word to either Chara's mother or her brother, he slipped his hand around Chara's waist and lifted her to one side, away from the others. "Ah, that's better. Now . . . have dinner with me tonight."

14

"No," Chara stated. "Excuse me, Mr. Wainwright, I must—"

"Call me Q. Everyone does, or at least call me Quent. All right, so we don't have dinner. I'll take you to a party," he said softly, the silver eyes amused at her mounting ire.

"What is the matter with you, Mr. Wainwright? Can't you take no for an answer?"

"Not usually."

"Well, take it as *the* answer now. Surely there are many young things here today who would be delighted to accompany you anywhere," Chara hissed, trying to wriggle free of the grip on her waist.

"Yes, I'm sure there are, but I don't want them. I want you." His eyes lavaed over her as he spoke.

Chara had the feeling her skin was being peeled. She wrenched free of his hold and made her way back to a bemused Ken. Her mother must have joined her other guests, Chara surmised as she looked around her.

At her urging, she and Ken left early. Chara vowed to give her mother and her friends a wide berth in the future.

Much to Chara's dismay, Quentin Wainwright began to call her. She hung up on him every time. Once, when he came to her apartment, she tried to close the door on him. He calmly announced he would kick it in unless she opened it. When she did, it was a repeat of her mother's party. This time, when she continued to refuse him, he turned rock hard, his eyes fiery. Before he left her apartment, he hauled her against him, grinding her lips into her teeth until she tasted blood in her mouth. Chara felt assaulted. The helpless anger was accompanied by a weak, fluttery feeling that was alien to her. She had been kissed many times in her twenty-five years, but she had never felt such an aftereffect.

But the mixture of happiness and pain that she ex-

15

perienced at not hearing from Quentin in over a week confused her.

When Ken called at the end of the week, she was sharp with him.

"What's the matter, Chara?" Ken asked, his own voice sounding strained.

At once Chara put her feelings in limbo and asked her brother what was wrong. At first he said he had to see her to talk about it. Then, as though he couldn't help himself, he blurted everything out to her on the phone. He had taken money from the petty cash box to cover some gambling debts he had incurred. He had been found out. Quentin told Ken he was coming to see Chara about it. Maybe it could be handled.

"Please, Chara, please, help me. I know it was stupid. Help me, Chara. I could be put in jail," Ken begged.

"How much?" Chara asked, knowing it would be more than she had somehow, already feeling Quentin's hands around her neck, squeezing.

"Ten thousand . . . or so," Ken muttered. When he heard Chara gasp, he hurried on. "Listen, Chara, I'll never do it again. I mean that. Just listen to what Quentin has to say. Help me, Chara."

Later that evening when she answered her door, Quent stood there, his face implacable, waiting until she asked him inside. He looked over her tiny apartment, his face telling her nothing.

"Would you like to sit down, Mr. Wainwright?" Chara asked, her words stilted as she tried to mask her nervousness.

"Yes. I'll sit down, but, first, I think we should get right to it. I have no intention of mincing words with you, Chara. I want you. Your brother is headed for jail without my intervention. I get *you*. He gets free. Well?" Quentin kept his eyes on her as he touched a lighter to a thick black cigar.

16

"God, you're an arrogant bastard," Chara blurted out, anger bubbling inside her.

Quentin bit down hard on the cigar, his eyes gray stone. "You can say no without the melodrama. Is it no, Chara? Do I leave here and let your brother go to jail?" Quentin snarled.

"No," Chara answered. "Release Ken. Then I'll be your, your . . ." Chara stumbled over the word.

"Mistress is the word, angel. I'll untangle Ken from his . . . er . . . predicament when we reach Las Vegas and you have kept your part of the bargain," Quentin said coldly. "That way there will be less temptation for you to cut and run." He turned toward the door and paused, his back to her. "Take the hangdog look off your face, Chara. There will be compensations. You'll find me more generous than most men you've known." He opened the door.

"Wait. How long do we keep up this charade?" Chara asked hoarsely, her tongue wetting her dry lips.

"As long as it takes, angel, until we tire of each other. Now get your act together. We leave tomorrow," Quentin pronounced flatly.

"Tomorrow?" Chara squeaked. "I can't. My job . . ."

"Tomorrow, Chara. You'll figure out something," Quent grated, reaching to pull her against his chest and dropping a punishing kiss on her mouth. "That's to remind you not to call me names."

Las Vegas was a city of light—light that hurt the eyes, day or night. The Learjet trip, the signing in at the prestigious Caesars had all been a blur to Chara. The tension had been building in her all day. She didn't know how she was going to go through with it. She knew that Quentin thought she was experienced by the remarks he had made to her. How she wished now that she had slept with Sid Marsh when he had nagged at her about it. Perhaps if she

17

hadn't discovered that he was really interested in meeting her mother, she might have finally succumbed to his relentless pressure. He had been the only one she had ever remotely considered going to bed with. She stood looking at herself in the full-length mirror in the bedroom of the suite Quentin had procured for them. Chara wasn't totally unaware of her looks. She had never wanted for boyfriends. She knew that the thick, straight, pale blond hair that she twisted into a chignon most often was appealing. Her rounded figure with the long slender legs often invited appreciative glances from men. Her porcelain skin, tanned a pale gold from the California sun, was a foil for the deep blue of her eyes. It was a personal cross to her that she was always taken for much younger than her age. *Soon that will be changed around,* she thought ruefully, as she studied her reflection. *Soon I'll have the sophisticated veneer of the resident mistress,* she informed her image with grim humor.

Her dress, grape-colored silk in the Grecian style, clung to her figure, outlining the thrust of her braless breasts. A gold butterfly clip held the one strap to her right shoulder. Her only other jewelry was a pair of gold hoops through her ears. Her shoes were gold slides, the heels high. A thin gold belt cinched her narrow waist; the hemline of her dress swirled to her knee. It was a far more expensive ensemble than she was used to wearing. She wondered how Quentin had managed to get her size in everything he had purchased for her and get it delivered to Caesars in time for their arrival.

He knocked once and came into her room.

As she turned to look at him, she hated him. She wanted to strike at him, to tear at him with nails that echoed the pale plum of her lipstick. She hated his twanging accent; his tall, dark looks with the black curling hair edging his collar; the deep tan. His wide shoulders and the long,

18

muscled legs were an affront to her. *Macho man,* she gritted to herself, *big phony, macho man.*

"You look beautiful, angel, but murderous. Try putting a smile on your face, would you? Let's go. I hope you like to gamble," he said, one eyebrow raised. "Then we'll dance a little if you like." He took her arm, leading her to the door.

"I'd like to eat. I'm hungry," Chara muttered.

"Dinner it is, then. Never let it be said that I didn't feed you . . . first." He laughed when Chara glared at him. "I'm hungry myself. Who knows, maybe the food will put you in a better mood," Quentin drawled, leaning down to brush his lips against Chara's neck, laughing again when she stiffened and tried to pull away. "Get used to it, Chara," he rasped, sharp teeth biting her earlobe, which sent waves of weakness through her. "I love your body and I'll be touching it often. Come on. It's going to be a long and lovely night and I promise you that the last part will be the best."

Chara was sure she would hate every minute of it, that her wobbling legs would give way under her, that she wouldn't be able to stop thinking about that last part that was ahead of her.

The food Quentin ordered was French and ambrosial. Delicate red snapper *en croute* with a piquante sauce, a spinach salad made crunchy with sunflower seeds and crisp bacon. To finish was either an elegant bombe or a cheese and fruit board. Chara refused the bombe and nibbled a grape with her coffee. The high-powered floor show seemed like a godsend to Chara. She could stop thinking for a short span of time.

When Quentin guided Chara to the gaming rooms, she confessed she had never gambled.

"That's surprising. Totally unlike your mother, I would say," Quentin said. "I understand from people in the in-

19

dustry that your father was a pretty high flyer as well. Ken seems to take after them, but not you, I guess, umm?"

"There has to be a black sheep in every family, Mr. Wainwright—"

"Do you think you can call me Quent now?" he interrupted, his fingers kneading her waist.

"And I'm the black sheep in ours," Chara continued, trying to pry his hands from her body. "I spent all my time in chapel saying my beads," she snapped.

Quentin's shout of laughter turned few of the heads bent in total absorption over the tables. It sent a ripple of pleasure down Chara's spine.

He placed some chips in her hand. Then all at once she had a pair of dice in her hand and several inquiring glances were turned her way.

"Throw them, Chara," Quentin whispered, his body pressed close to her back.

The next two hours were a flurry of winning and losing. Chara knew she was winning only by the shouts of approval; the groans told her when she was losing. She began echoing her gallery. She laughed and applauded when the point was hers. She sighed and pouted when the house won.

Flushed and laughing, she allowed Quentin to pour a stream of chips into her purse. "Did I win all those? Where may I cash them in? No, I don't want to play anymore." Chara shook her head. "No, Quent, I can cash them in myself. You said you wanted to play for a bit. When I'm through changing my chips, I'll find you."

Quentin shrugged, putting his lighter to the thin cheroot in his mouth, then flicking one finger against her cheek. "All right, Chara. Don't be long. I'll be at the roulette table, over there." Quentin jerked his head toward a very quiet but crowded area. Chara knew just by his actions that he was probably quite familiar with most of the gambling tables.

She nodded and left him. At the cashier's window she had no trouble explaining to the man that she wanted her winnings sent to the nearest relief station for battered children. The man didn't change expression when she emptied her purse. She filled in the draft and gave it to the unsmiling man in the cage. He assured her it would be mailed. Satisfied, she decided to walk around the huge club before she returned to Quentin. After a few minutes she was so confused by the noise and press of people that she decided to find him at once.

"Pardon me. You look lost. Will you let me buy you a drink?" A tall, pale-skinned man with light hair was standing in front of her. Even to Chara's untrained eye his brown suit was of an impeccable cut. She started to shake her head no, but he forestalled her by taking out a leather wallet. "Don't say no. I have a great deal of identification. I'm a businessman of good repute," he argued. He looked at her left hand. "I can see you're not married. What would be wrong in just having one drink?"

Chara smiled at his plaintive tone. Before she could say that she didn't think she would because she was with someone, a cold voice spoke behind her. "The lady's with me. Don't come near her again."

Chara turned to see the red run under Quent's skin, the rocklike mask of his face barely concealing his rage. "It's all right, Quent, I . . ." Chara began, lifting one hand placatingly.

"Never mind, come with me," Quentin snarled, taking her arm in a steel grip. Chara didn't look at the pale-skinned man again, but she could feel his gaze on her. Anger rose in her at Quentin's manner. She allowed him to lead her blindly from the gambling rooms. She had no idea of their destination. She didn't notice her surroundings. Her only awareness was her own bubbling wrath.

When Quentin seated her at a table, she blinked. There was music and a dance floor. He must have ordered for

21

them because all at once there was a glass of champagne in front of her. She gulped it down and it was refilled.

"Don't drink it like it was soda or you'll be flat on your back. I thought you weren't much of a drinker. Or was that just one of your cutesy put-ons?" Quentin bit down on his cigar, then mashed it in the ashtray, an angry sheen to his eyes.

"I am usually a very light drinker, but I have discovered that you're easier to take if I'm loaded. Soooo . . ." She lifted her glass and quaffed the contents, the dry bubbles making her cough.

"Damn it, Chara, don't keep pushing, or I'll start pushing back. Come on, we're going to dance," Quent ordered, his one hand lifting her from the chair.

As Chara wended her way through the tables, she had to fight to keep steady; the champagne had made her light-headed.

Quentin pulled her hard against him, making her breathless for a moment. "Damn you, Chara, you're tipsy. What's with you anyway?"

"I'll tell you what's with me, Mr. Wonderful. I'm bloody furious." Chara hiccuped, her anger boiling at the amused gleam in Quentin's eyes. "And take that damn smirk off your face, you . . . you . . ."

"Keep your voice down, Chara," Quentin drawled, his mouth close to her ear as he bent over her, laughter threading his voice.

"I won't," Chara mumbled, aware of smiling stares turned their way. She closed her eyes and turned her face into his shoulder, trying to concentrate on the voice of the satin-clad songstress as she throbbed out a love song. Because Chara had a secret love of all romantic ballads, she didn't speak until the singer had switched to another song. "I did not try to pick up that man. He thought I was alone and offered me a drink," Chara said, feeling less rocky the longer they danced.

"I know what he was offering you, Chara," Quentin said, his voice hard. "There will be no other men now, Chara. You belong to me."

"I belong to *me,*" Chara said, erupting. "Besides, I was about to tell him that I was with someone else."

"I came along and saved you the trouble, angel. Just remember what I said, Chara. You're mine now," Quentin growled, his teeth grazing her cheek before fastening to her earlobe.

Chara pulled back from him, breathless, wishing he wouldn't do that to her. She cursed him for making her feel like a helpless teen-ager. "I don't feel like dancing anymore," she muttered.

"Fine," Quentin said, leading her from the floor. He dealt with the bill with a flourish of his pen, then cupped her elbow to take her from the floor.

It wasn't until they were almost to their suite that Chara realized her predicament. She faltered, edging away from Quentin's restraining hold. "I . . . I think I would like more champagne."

Quentin looked down at her, his face still, before the slow smile lifted the corners of his mouth. "Really? All right. I don't think you need it, but if you insist, I'll have some sent to our suite." He watched her like an eagle with a fieldmouse as he turned the key in the lock, then pushed the door open. "Come on, Chara. No more stalling." His voice was a cynical purr. "It's time to pay the piper."

"You cold-hearted bastard." Chara gasped as he propelled her into the room and kicked it shut behind them.

"Stop talking like a tough." His nostrils flared in irritation, his black brows snapping together over his nose. "Now, which shower do you want? Or would you rather we took one together?" He let his smile run over her, making Chara's skin burn.

"Wait, Quent, I have to talk to you." Chara gulped, red-faced.

23

"No more manuvers, Chara. I'm not in the mood for those kinds of games. I have something more interesting in mind," Quent drawled, removing his tie, then letting it fall to the floor. Chara watched its descent, mesmerized, feeling more threatened than she could ever remember. "And don't get any ideas about copping out on me, lady. I'll come after you, and you won't like it. Now get along. I'm not a patient man."

"Quent, please." She moistened her lips, trying to swallow around the lump in her throat. "There's something I have to tell you, something you should know about me. I—"

"Chara," he interrupted, "I don't know what your game is, but let me tell you right now, I won't be jerked around. Don't try to hustle the hustler, lady. It can't be done. I think I told you the game is over. Now get ready." Every word was chopped out as though he were a general giving orders to his army.

"You don't tell me what to do," Chara shouted at him, diverted from her objective by what she considered his tyrannical treatment of her. "Who do you think you are? I don't need you—"

"You're wrong there, Chara," Quentin bellowed back. "You do need me if you want to keep that brother of yours out of prison."

"That's right, keep reminding me," Chara said back to him, her chin thrust forward. "You're no gentleman."

"I never claimed to be one."

"It's a good thing, because you're not," she riposted, wishing she could take the Steuben vase from the table and crash it down on his head. "I'm sorry my brother ever went to work for you."

"I can't say that I've been happy about the association. It certainly doesn't add to my peace of mind to have a thief on the payroll," Quentin rasped, his silver eyes dangerous.

"Don't you dare say that about Kenny," Chara

squeaked, her temper heating up. "How dare you!" She launched herself at him, wanting to scratch his eyes out.

He fended off her attack by gripping her wrists in a punishing hold, not seeming to care that he was close to breaking her bones. They glared at each other, anger vibrating between them like a loose hot wire. He shoved her backward so that she collapsed on the bed. "Take a shower, Chara. I'll talk to you then." He went through to the other room, slamming the door behind him.

"Wait," she mumbled to the closed door. "I'm twenty-five years old and a virgin. Isn't that a kick in the head?" She stared straight ahead of her for some moments, her mind totally blank.

When she realized how much time she was wasting, she almost tore the grape silk from her body.

Still a bundle of nerves because she couldn't figure how to tell Quentin that she was one of the endangered species, a virgin, she opted to soak in the bathtub for a short time instead of taking a shower. Perhaps inspiration would come from a steaming soak. Her attention caught by the round sunken tub, she smiled to herself, thinking what a Cleopatra scene it was. Impulsively she added lavish amounts of the sweet-smelling bath salts that sat on the shelf as she turned the gold spigots on full. The combination of steam and perfumed water lulled her. When the water cooled, she added more. Drowsy and relaxed, she lay back, easing her head onto the soft bath pillow. Her body floated free in the deep water. Her lids grew very heavy.

She felt a sudden draft of air. As her eyelids lifted she was too bemused to do more than watch as Quentin lowered himself onto the tub beside her. Blinking, she tried to straighten up, but he was too fast for her, pulling her close to his hair-rough chest.

"Lovely, angel; I wish I had thought of it. What a sweet and subtle way of inviting me into your tub, letting me come and find you here," Quentin husked, his hands running over her wet, silken body. They seemed to float against one another. One of Quentin's thumbs gently stroked Chara's nipple, making her gasp.

"Get out of here. I didn't want you in here, Quent." She choked as she felt his other hand kneading her thigh.

"Oh, you wanted me in here, Chara. I'm sure of it. Believe me, I'm not quarreling with the technique, sweetheart." He groaned as he lifted her body free of the water for a moment, to take one breast into his mouth.

Chara couldn't breathe. She had no strength; she had no will. If Quentin released her now, she was sure she would just sink to the bottom of the tub and drown.

His eyes deepened to the color of old pewter as he lifted his head to look at her parted lips. "Chara . . ." he murmured as he bent his head to claim her mouth. "Chara," he gasped when her hands grasped his shoulders. Without taking his mouth from hers, he lifted her into his arms and lowered her onto the thick carpeting that surrounded the tub area.

Chara's senses were reeling. The small voice that told her to stop Quentin was being smothered by the rising tide of feeling that threatened to swamp her. Other men had tried to make love to her and she had turned them aside easily, not once losing the cool detachment that allowed her to make the choice. She had expected savagery from Quentin Wainwright. Perhaps she could have withstood that. His gentle attack disarmed her. She responded without thought, her body feeling warm, silky, weak.

Quentin's mouth left Chara's to travel slowly down the column of her neck. He stopped for a moment to nip at one earlobe, sending a weakness stabbing through her. Chara's head rolled, her glazed eyes seeing the steam rising from the tub as a cocoon for her and Quentin.

When she felt his lips close again around one moist

nipple, she was sure she was coming apart in chunks. Chara groaned, her body arching toward him.

His hands moved with gentle certainty across her middle, sliding upward to caress her throat, then caressing downward, his mouth following his hands as though he would doubly brand her. She was his. He was telling her this, and she wasn't fighting his decision. His hands and mouth became more urgent.

Chara's senses sharpened even as the world receded. She knew that she would regret this, but she didn't care. The smell of the bath salts that clung to both their bodies was pungent to her nose. She could see each damp, curling strand of Quentin's jet black hair. The ragged joy of their breathing seemed symphony loud. She was on fire with a longing to be closer to him, to belong to him.

He drew back his head, his breathing as labored as her own. "I want you like hell, Chara. I've never wanted anyone more. Can you feel how much I want you, angel?" Quentin asked gently, leaning over her, his tongue stroking her cheek.

Too weak to answer, Chara nodded, pulling his head down to her again. "Be kind to me, Quent. Please be gentle," she whispered.

"Angel." Quentin's hot eyes were quizzical for a moment. Then he folded her closer with a low growl. "Of course I'll be gentle with you, love."

And he was, coaxing her to such a level that she became impatient with him. She begged him to love her, not even knowing that she did it. Her fingernails gouged his shoulders as her fevered body reacted to each deep kiss, each stroking caress. When he lifted himself over her, she was eager for him.

The spasm of pain caused her to cry out. She felt Quentin stiffen for a moment, his eyes narrowing on her, then he was kissing her and moving with increasing urgency. When the explosion came, Chara felt as though they had fallen off the world. She spiraled into a kaleidoscope of feeling.

Still locked in his arms, she felt herself lifted, her breath slowly coming back to normal as Quentin eased her over on top of his body, his inscrutable gaze probing hers. "Are you all right, Chara?"

"Tired." Chara yawned, one hand ineffectually trying to mask the yawn, but one came right after the other.

"I'd better get you to bed, angel," Quentin said, his smile rueful as he watched Chara's eyelids close. "We'll talk about the changes in our plans tomorrow," he stated, lifting her as though she were a doll.

A sleepy Chara thought she felt those arms tighten on her possessively, but she couldn't be sure. Shivering a little as he put her between the sheets, she thought how well they had dried each other with their bodies. Almost purring, Chara snuggled into his chest, sighing with satisfaction as those arms closed around her. Through the haze of sleep she reveled in the tingling well-being of her body. Her last thought was that she finally understood what all those love poems and romantic novels were talking about. She smiled, kissed Quentin's chest, and slept.

Hot desert sun made a pattern through the figured sheers, waking Chara, the strange room puzzling her for a moment. The memory of last night rushed in on her, making her pull back. The motion brought the realization that she was still locked tight in Quentin's arms. As she looked up into his face, his sleep-filled eyes opened, focusing on her at once.

"Hello." Chara blushed, wishing she knew another more apt greeting for the man who was her lover. When she tried to ease backward on the bed, Quentin's arm tightened.

"Good morning, Chara. How do you feel?" Quentin asked.

28

"Fine." She colored as his eyes probed her face. It seemed to Chara that he was looking for something. She felt self-conscious under that stare and felt that she had to escape. "I . . . ah . . . I think I'll take a shower."

"Will you now?" Quentin drawled, giving her a one-sided smile that made her heart drop in her chest and bounce back to its original position again. "Shall I wash your back?"

Chara could feel her eyes widening on him as his one hand stroked her bare hip. "Oh, I don't think that's necessary. I have to wash my hair . . . and it will be boring for you." Chara winced at her choice of words.

Quentin's black brow arched, then he shook his head. "Boring for me? No, I don't think so . . . but we'd never get out of there today. I'll take a kiss though." He crushed her close to him, so that she was pressed along his entire length. His mouth sought hers, and a seductive tongue probed her mouth. She felt his heart accelerate as her own tongue gently touched his. He pulled her back with a gasp. "God, Chara. I have to go. I have something to do this morning, but I'll be back for lunch. Wear something dressy, not casual." He rose from the bed, naked. Chara could hardly take her eyes from him. He donned his brown terry robe and left the room without looking at her or saying anything else.

Chara felt rebuffed. *Don't be a fool,* she argued with herself, *he's probably sick of you already. You'll be free of him.* Dully she wondered why this thought didn't make her happy as she pushed open the door to the bathroom. As she looked at the sunken tub, last night came back with a rush. Heat suffused her body as she remembered how abandoned her responses were to the man she professed to hate. *God,* she thought as she pressed a shaking hand to her forehead, *no wonder he wants to be rid of me.* Not able to bear taking a bath, she contented herself with a quick shower and washed her hair. Though she dawdled over

29

everything, even the croissants and coffee she ordered for breakfast, she still had time to spare before Quentin would be returning for lunch. Perhaps he wouldn't even feel like eating with her, she thought, feeling sorry for herself. Rummaging through her luggage, she found the bikini and silky one-piece suit she had stuffed there. She opted for the bikini, reasoning it would give her more exposure to the sun. She would swim and sun until Quentin decided to send her back to L.A.

There were few people at the pool so early in the day. One woman approached her and asked if she could borrow Chara's suntan oil since she had left hers in her room. It amused Chara that the woman also expected her to rub some on her back. Chara complied good-naturedly. When the gray-haired man, who seemed to be the woman's companion, came over and tried to strike up a conversation with Chara, the woman decided she had had enough of Chara's lotion and led her friend away. Chara looked around her, her attention caught by another woman Chara judged to be in her forties, who was already lathered with oil, her glistening, leatherlike skin a cocoa brown. One balding, pot-bellied man ogled Chara as she chose a lounge chair far removed from the other two. For a moment, as she wriggled under the man's stare, she wondered if she shouldn't have worn a one-piece suit instead of the two polka-dotted blue hankie-sized pieces she was wearing. Then she shrugged, fixed goggles to her eyes to protect them from the chlorine, and lowered herself into the water. Her long-reaching, easy crawl carried her up and down the regulation-sized pool. After twenty laps, she lifted herself breathless onto the side, then, moving her chair into the shade, she chose a magazine from the assortment on a table and began to read. Before long the printed page was dancing and she put it aside and closed her eyes.

"Why didn't you leave a note telling me where you were?" Quentin's harsh voice startled her awake.

Lifting her knuckles to her eyes, she rubbed, not answering him at first. "I was only going to be out here a minute. What time is it?" Chara mumbled, fumbling for her towel, feeling uneasy as Quentin's hard-eyed look raked her body.

"It's after twelve. I looked all over. I thought maybe you had left, but I was sure you would have taken at least one suitcase with you." He growled, pushing aside her legs and sitting down on the lounger, unbuttoning his shirt even more than it was in the heat.

"Where would I have gone?" Chara asked, puzzled.

"How the hell do I know?" Quentin rasped. "Come on, it's time to get dressed. Otherwise we'll be late. When I told you to wear something dressy, I should have known your darn contrariness would make you grab for a bikini, if that's what you call those scraps of material," Quentin scolded, scowling down the length of her. "God, Chara, don't you know the men around this pool can't take their eyes off you? Are you asking for a riot? Would it make you happy to see me in a brawl?" he snarled, his hand grazing her skin as he moved it to place it on the other side of the lounger.

"Why you, you . . ." Chara sputtered, bringing herself forward, forgetting for a moment that she had untied her bra top. "You are a pompous ass, Quentin Wainwright. Oooh." She and Quentin reached for the falling bikini top at the same time. His knuckles touched her breast and she could feel it tauten in response.

"Damn you, Chara," he ground through his teeth, his face turning red as he stared at her uncovered breasts, then at the poolside residents openly ogling her. "Get something on. *Now.*" Enraged, he threw ugly, contorted glances at the people near them, then threw a towel around her and pulled her to her feet, almost dragging her from the area.

Chara was quite aware of the many interested stares

31

that followed them. She waited only long enough for the door to their suite to be closed before she rounded on Quentin, fury choking her. "Where the hell—"

"Don't talk tough, Chara."

"Don't you interrupt me," she squealed, shaking her fist at him, allowing the towel that was wrapped toga-style around her to slip. She tried to hitch it up, still berating Quentin. All at once she realized his eyes were darkening to a storm-cloud gray. Before she could back away he had snatched the towel from her and pulled her into his arms, dropping his hard mouth onto hers with a groan.

"Kiss me, Chara," he growled against her mouth, his tongue teasing her lower lip.

For a moment she resisted, then went limp against him, reminding herself that this would be all she would have of Quentin. He would send her away today, she was sure. "Quent," she pleaded, kissing him as she had never before, clinging and abandoned, feeling his heart thunder against her. Reveling in the knowledge that she had the power to arouse him, as he was arousing her, she sighed and let her fingers lift to unbutton his shirt.

He pulled back, his strong mouth shaking, his face white under the dark tan. "No, damn you, Chara, no. God knows I want to take you right to that bed, but we can't."

"Why?" She pouted, feeling reckless.

"Because we're getting married in less than an hour," Quentin answered tersely, holding her by her upper arms and turning her toward the bathroom. "Close your mouth, angel, you'll catch flies," he mocked softly, then patted her sharply on the backside. "Now get dressed. Wear something pretty. I love your bikini, but I think it's a little informal for our marriage ceremony."

CHAPTER TWO

She stared through the window, not really seeing the lush green golf course that pushed its way into the desert or even her own dazed reflection sketched on the glass. *I'm not Chara Styles anymore,* she thought numbly, *I'm Chara Wainwright.*

"Regretting the union already, bride?" Quentin growled, his lips grazing Chara's neck.

She started, her eyes lifting to stare at the image that had joined hers in the glass. She had not heard Quentin approach, but even with closed eyes she would have recognized the now familiar sardonic tones. She wondered for a moment if there was anything he wasn't cynical about, this new husband, of one hour, of hers. It struck her as the height of irony that he was everything she most disliked in a man—sophisticated, world-weary, harsh—and now she was married to him. Why? Why did he give her this unsettled feeling, that she was hot and cold at the same time? Why hadn't she struggled against him when he had told her they were being married? What was wrong with her that she so easily gave herself, body and soul, to a man she despised?

"Come along, Chara, we're leaving now," Quentin told her, leading her away from his friends who had insisted they have a drink after the wedding in the chapel. Chara had no idea where Quentin had found the friends to stand up with them. She had no idea how he had arranged the chapel or the minister. She moved like an automaton and made her responses the same way.

When they were back in their suite she called Ken and listened to his jubilant ravings with a jaundiced ear. "Listen, Chara, he's loaded. He'd never have to work if he didn't choose. The family is in all sorts of things . . . electronics, maybe, I'm not sure. His movies are all moneymakers. Just think, now he's my brother-in-law. Mother will blow a gasket." Ken chortled. "In fact, if you don't mind, Chara, I'd like to be the one to tell her."

Chara winced at her brother's glee but was secretly glad that she wouldn't have to speak with her mother.

"Chara? Chara, are you listening? What do you think old Kermit and Agnes will think when they hear you've tied the knot. You can be sure Mother will be quick to inform them that since you are under thirty and have married, that small legacy father left you, with that stipulation, will now become yours. I'm sure they considered that tidy bundle all their own. You have really shook the bushes this time, sister mine. By the way, speaking of people in England, won't you want to be calling Wendy and telling her? After all, you roomed with her that one year you spent there in college," Kenny burbled.

After Chara assured him that she would contact her friend and once again assured him that he was in the clear as far as the discrepancy at the studio, she adjured him to keep to the straight and narrow, then broke the connection.

Quentin broke into her reverie by offering her a glass of champagne. "You hardly seem the blushing, excited bride, Mrs. Wainwright. Is it because we anticipated our vows last night?" Quentin queried, the smile not touching his hard eyes.

More hurt than she could ever admit, Chara lashed out. "Don't you patronize me, Quent. I'm keeping my side of the bargain. Marriage was your idea, not mine."

"So it was. Drink your champagne, Chara," he snapped, turning away from her to fill his own glass. Keeping his back to her, he continued speaking, his drawl very pronounced. "How is it you neglected to tell me, lovely wife, that you were, as the old-time writers used to say, untouched?" Quentin tipped some champagne into his mouth, then turned to rivet her with those silver eyes.

Chara swallowed, lifting her eyes to meet his stare with an effort, unaware that her eyes had deepened to violet. "I tried . . . to tell you before we . . . before I took my bath. You wouldn't listen. Then . . . well . . ."

"Yes. Things did get out of hand," Quentin said, his voice cold. "Why the hell didn't you make me listen. I'm not in the habit of . . . of . . ." Now he floundered, gulping more champagne.

"I know what you mean, Mr. Wonderful," Chara hissed, angry humiliation coursing through her body. "I should be ashamed to be a virgin in this enlightened age. Right? No, don't interrupt me. I know damn well that the ratio of virgins over twenty is small, but I'll tell you something. I didn't choose to change that until I was black-mailed into it by an unscrupulous director too used to having his own way." Chara paused for breath, air shooting through her windpipe. "I . . . I wish I had been VD queen of L.A., Mr. Big Shot. Now why don't we call this big farce quits." She hiccupped, swiping a hand at her eyes and trying to make a dash for the bathroom.

Before she had taken two steps, a steel-muscled arm pulled her back. She struggled against him, knocking the glass of champagne from his hand. Hearing his muffled curse, Chara redoubled her efforts to be free to no avail.

"Damn it, Chara, be still. You could step on that glass and shatter it. Why it didn't break I'll never know. Now be quiet and listen to me. Nothing has changed, except now we're married. You're as much mine now as you were before, more so in the eyes of the world. We stay together," Quentin grated in her ear, his palm rubbing her flat stomach, as though to soothe her stiffened body. "Now I want you to get dressed. We'll go out for our wedding dinner. Tomorrow we'll be leaving Vegas."

"Are we going back to L.A.?" Chara bit her lip to keep it from trembling, knowing that her ragged breathing increased as Quentin held her closer.

"No, lovely wife. We're going on our honeymoon. I have a hideaway in central New York State. I want you to see it. I haven't been there in quite a while myself. Now go and get dressed." He patted her on the backside and went to his own room.

Chara didn't move, her hands going first to her face, then rubbing her arms, then twisting around. It seemed as though her twitching fingers were drawing her eye more and more to the wide band of gold that adorned her third finger almost to the knuckle. Like a slave bracelet, she thought, gulping back an angry sob.

Not caring what she wore, she took the first dress she touched, rummaging for shoes to match the black tissue silk. Chara, who up to now had had one silk blouse that she tenderly cared for, suddenly had a closetful of silks in every color. A clothes lover all her life, Chara would have been ecstatic with them at any other time. Now she felt nothing as she showered, shampooed, rubbed her body with the Joy cream perfume, then donned sheer black bikini panties and ultrasheer black pantyhose. The stockings defined the shapeliness of her slender legs, emphasizing her ankles when she slipped on the peau de soie slides. She wore no bra because the dress plunged in a V back and front.

Her eyes widened as she looked into the full-length mirror, wondering if the dress was too daring, if the rope of hair coiled on top of her head made her too tall.

"God, Chara, you're lovely. Here. I want you to wear these." Quentin's husky voice spoke from the door. Before she could turn, he was there behind her. "You have a curving body that's delectable, wife, and I love those sapphire eyes. What man could ask for more?" Quentin placed tiny kisses across her shoulder and up her neck, making her quiver.

"I don't want the necklace and earrings." Chara gulped. "I won't take anything from you. Is this what you did for your other mistresses?"

"You're not my mistress, Chara. You're my wife. Now hold still. This chain is so fine my fingers can hardly handle it. There. You can put the earrings on yourself. You look devastating, Chara, sculpted in pink pearl." He breathed loudly, turning her in his arms.

Trembling, Chara licked her lips, not wanting him to see how his closeness affected her. "How predictable you are! Buy her some trinkets and she'll roll over on her back for you." Chara gasped as his grip tightened. "Won't this marriage anger some of the others waiting in the harem? Oww, don't! You're hurting me."

"I'll do more than hurt you if you don't learn to control that acid tongue of yours," Quentin grated, his eyes raking her over. "Then again, I don't see this marriage interfering with my life too much. Do you?"

"You're disgusting," Chara sputtered, struggling to break his hold. "Nothing is sacred to your kind. I can't bear the thought of being your wife."

"It doesn't matter what you think of me. You *are* my wife and I'm telling you to watch that tongue," he rasped, then yanked her closer so that she lost her breath. When she opened her mouth to gulp air, he fastened his mouth to it, the sudden exploration shocking her. She felt taken, possessed, once more. No matter how she fought it, the stirrings in her lower body started a heat in the core of her that turned to furnace temperature.

Quentin broke free first, lifting her chiffon wrap around her shoulders and handing her her jet beaded bag. Chara cursed his equanimity.

Dinner and dancing were a blur. She promised herself she would not respond to him, but before they left the cabaret to go back to their suite, Quentin's lovemaking on the dance floor had reduced her to jelly. When he came to her room that night, she tried to fight him off. Within minutes she was groaning his name, her hands threaded through his crisp black hair. She hardly heard his shaken, triumphant laugh as he folded her closer, his mouth roving her body.

Twice more in the night he woke her. Each time she turned to him eagerly.

Very early the next morning they were aloft in the Learjet that Quentin informed her belonged to his family's company.

Chara closed her eyes, aware of a vague relief that she was flying away from her mother's vicinity and not toward it. She refused to think of the aloof man riding opposite her, apart from her and engrossed in the papers he had taken from his briefcase. To Chara's inexperienced eye it looked like a script he was reading. Each time she looked at him she remembered with appalling clarity her eager, passionate responses to his lovemaking the previous night. With effort she was able to concentrate on the telephone conversation she had had before dinner with Wendy Millar, the exchange student from Alsace-Lorraine, whom she had roomed with when they had both been on scholarship at the London Institute for the Humanities.

"Chara, darling, you can't be married! Not after all the vows you made never to give yourself to a man. Oh, never mind." Wendy laughed. "I don't care. As long as you're happy. Make him bring you to London. Raoul and I are no longer together, so I just rattle around here by myself. Be happy, love . . ."

Chara smiled to herself as she thought of her dark-haired, dark-eyed friend who bounced through life with unbridled enthusiasm. She turned her head to look out the plane window, her eyelids heavy.

She hardly moved when they stopped for a short time. Chara assumed it was to refuel. She sunk back in her seat into a deep sleep.

She felt something pushing at her and tried to snuggle deeper into her seat. Her lids were lead as she lifted them in response to the whispered command. She wasn't in her bed as she had thought. She blinked upward at Quentin, all at once aware that she was tucked close to his chest and that she was very comfortable.

"Isn't it nice to waken in your husband's arms?" Quentin said mockingly into her ear.

Chara straightened, pushing away from him, trying to smooth the cotton skirt that had gathered up over her hips while she slept. She looked away from that twist of a smile.

"Come along, wife. Take your small case. One of the men from the company has the rest of our things. We'll just take what we need for two days. We'll do some shopping in New York and see a couple of shows. Would you like that?" When Chara nodded, he grinned. Chara gulped at the blatant charm of the man. "Have you ever visited New York, Chara?"

"Just the airport. When I was in school in Rochester we sometimes had a stopover of an hour or so here and I flew from here to London when I went to school there, but I've never seen the city," Chara said, interested in spite of herself. "At what hotel are we staying?"

"No hotel. I have an apartment overlooking Central Park. I think you'll like it," Quentin said, taking it for granted when a taxi was procured for them at once. "New

39

York is a great city, Chara, but you really need a guide to see the real New York. I'll be yours."

Before she could ascertain if he was mocking her again, the taxi driver sailed away from the curb, beginning one of the most hair-raising events of Chara's life, a cab ride into Manhattan. Chara was sure the driver had no brakes. The third time she was thrown against Quentin as the cab dodged another car, she didn't try to move away. At once Quentin clamped Chara tight to his side. More than once she turned her face into his jacket rather than face the oncoming traffic. Somehow they weren't hit.

"Believe it or not, you'll get used to it, bride. All the cabbies in New York drive this way." Quentin laughed in her ear. "I certainly don't mind holding you in my arms." His chuckle angered Chara, but she stayed put rather than risk being tossed about like a ball.

She barely had time to glance at the stone facade of the apartment building before Quentin led her under the awning and through the door held open by a smiling uniformed man who nodded to Quentin. It surprised Chara when Quentin introduced her as his wife to the man before leading her to the elevator. Her stomach rose almost as rapidly as the elevator when she realized that she would soon be alone with her husband again.

She forgot everything as she studied the brown and cream elegance of the sunken living room that seemed almost too big to Chara. Her eyes were drawn to the sliding glass doors that led to a nearly as large terrace that held a swimming pool and, wonder of wonders, a vegetable garden.

"Crazy, isn't it?" Quentin laughed behind her. "I like fresh vegetables and my day help, a husband-and-wife team, decided on this. I like it. Feel free to pick anything—flowers, vegetables . . . or plant something if you wish."

Chara shook her head, very aware of Quentin's warm

hand resting at her waist. "I don't think I'll plant anything, but I like gardens. Maybe I'll have a tomato." Chara's voice was hoarse as she pulled free of his touch. Damn. What was the matter with her anyway?

"Come on, Chara, you can come back to the terrace later. Let me show you our rooms. I have to go downtown for a while. You can rest or swim or whatever you want. I'll have my secretary make reservations for dinner early, then we'll catch a show . . . then maybe dancing if you're not too tired. See you later."

Quentin dropped Chara's bag in a bedroom adjoining his own, leaned down, and gave her a hard kiss before she could recoil. Then he was gone. Chara rubbed shaking fingers across her mouth

After unpacking, she moved through the apartment, admiring the slick good taste that had furnished it. No expense had been spared to ensure comfort and ease. Delighted with the sauna in her bathroom, Chara promised herself she would make use of it, then lingered in the shower, washed her hair, shaved her legs, and rubbed her skin with the exotic skin lotions that abounded there. She grimaced at her worn terry-cloth robe, cursing the absentminded decision that had made her pack that in the small case instead of one of her new, silky ones. She hated to cover her exotic-smelling body with it. She took time with her makeup and was just adding a touch of blue mascara the color of her eyes when the doorbell rang. Startled, she tried not to think of all the stories she had read about crimes in New York.

When Chara answered on the intercom, the doorman informed her that he had sent up packages that had been delivered for her. Open-mouthed, Chara watched the messenger deposit boxes in the spacious foyer.

For a moment Chara hesitated, then, unable to restrain herself, she opened them. In one there was a note.

BRIDE, ENJOY. HOPE YOU LIKE MY TASTE. TOMOR-
ROW YOUR TURN. Q.

Chara stared at the note long moments before crum-
pling it. She was about to drop it into a wastebasket when
something made her smooth it out and place it in her robe
pocket.

The dress she pulled from the box marked Saks Fifth
Avenue was a whisper of sky blue chiffon with spaghetti
straps, molded tight across the bodice. The skirt fell from
a point under the breasts in full graceful folds, the hemline
uneven and fluid, reaching to just below her knee. Every
move Chara made flared the dress about her, giving her
rounded figure a sylphlike look. She slid the matching blue
leather slides onto her feet, the three-inch heels making
her a graceful five foot nine inches tall. She was ready far
too early, but as she twirled in front of the mirror in her
room, she was too delighted with her image to care.

"Well, well, well. It looks better than even I imagined
it would, angel," Quentin drawled from the doorway, his
hot silver eyes flowing over her. "I'll hurry and get ready.
What a nice contrast we'll make—Lucifer and the Madon-
na." Quentin's laugh trailed behind him.

Chara turned away from the mirror, irritated with herself because she was so pleased by Quentin's sudden appearance. She had not expected him for another hour. She
felt confused and restless by her response to him. She
walked from the room down the lushly carpeted hallway
to the short stairway that led to the lower level. She looked
neither left nor right as she passed through the elegant
sitting room and out onto the terrace. She had to think.
Somehow she had to fight against the hold that Quentin
was gaining on her. After all, hadn't she been a paralegal
with an analytical mind, she queried herself angrily. Many
times Sol Mannstein, her boss, had complimented her on

her logical approach to problems. Surely she could handle one man. He wasn't Superman, was he, she asked herself. Damn near it. She ground her teeth in frustration, trying not to listen to the answering voice. *Don't be a fool, Chara, you can fight this pseudo attraction. Don't forget what he'd be like if he ever finds out you're infatuated with him! What will he do? What can he do? Send me back to L.A.? That's all right. Sol said a job would be waiting for me. So why don't you feel happier about it?*

She put her hands over her ears, as though she could blot out the caustic voice in her mind. *I will not let him see what an effect he has on me,* she promised herself. *After all, those are just ordinary sexual responses that I would feel with any man,* she assured herself. *Liar! Damn that voice.*

She wriggled in discomfort as she leaned forward on the parapet. She glanced down at her full breasts rising from the tight blue bodice. For the first time in many a year she questioned if her dress might be cut too low. Usually that didn't bother her. Knowing that she had an attractive bustline that looked well in low cut dresses, she wore the latest styles with aplomb. She sighed and told herself not to be silly.

She tried to relax as she looked out over what many have termed the most exciting city in the world. She felt a stirring of anticipation as she thought about being out there that very evening. Quentin would be sure to know many of the celebrities in town. Disquiet touched Chara for a moment as she thought of all the fascinating people they might see. Quentin would see her as gauche in comparison with the sophisticated women they might meet. Chara lifted her chin in an unconscious gesture of defiance.

"Here." His voice crooned in her ear and he laughed when Chara jumped. "Relax, bride, and drink this. It's just some chilled Chablis. Quite a view, huh?"

She took the drink in her left hand and her right hand made a sweeping motion over the balcony. "It's wonderful. I'm anxious to see it." She pointed to another building. "I can see that there are others who have gardens on their terraces too. It's a nice idea." She cleared her throat, her eyes going to Quentin. "I like your apartment . . . all that I've seen anyway." She smiled at him but couldn't hold his gaze. His was too openly intimate. She sipped her wine, looking out over the city again.

"*Our* apartment, my sweet. Your key is sitting on your dresser. Here, let me take your glass. I want you to try this on," Quentin said softly before reaching into his jacket pocket and bringing forth a rectangular jeweler's box. "I think this will go with your dress. There are matching earrings in there as well. Turn around and let me fasten it for you."

Bemused, Chara obeyed, knowing she should refuse but not wanting to precipitate an argument when Quentin seemed to be in such a good mood. Her hand went up to the heart-shaped cluster of sapphires on a filigree chain. When Quentin took her hand and led her into the lounge so that she could see herself in the scrolled mirror, she didn't resist. He stood behind her as he watched her push the gold posts through her pierced earlobes. The earrings were gold filigree with a center sapphire. Chara tensed as she studied the face behind her in the mirror.

"You give me too much . . ." Chara began.

"I like giving you things. Husbands are supposed to do things like that." Quentin leaned down, his nostrils flaring as he inhaled her perfume.

"And I won't keep them when . . . when . . ." Chara replied.

"Suit yourself, Chara." Quent shrugged, his eyes silver agate. "These aren't heirlooms. Throw them away if you wish."

"That's awful." Chara gasped, hating the twist to his

mouth. "I suppose you are used to giving more expensive trinkets to all your other women?" she snapped.

Quentin grinned. Again Chara was taken aback by his forceful charm. "I'm known to be generous to the women that interest me, but I'm sure you have an exaggerated idea of the number of women that I have. By the way, where did such a modern, paralegal lady pick up such an old fashioned word as trinket?" Quentin drawled, taking her arm and leading her to the foyer, not even waiting for her answer as he pulled something from a box on a chair. "You'll need a wrap even though the night is mild. I picked this up from an old friend." He held out a cobwebby drift of shawl that looked much like the Maltese lace Chara and Wendy had seen once on a trip to the island. Quent smiled at the questioning look on her face. "It's a grandmother of a friend of mine who makes these. The family is from Portugal. Though she has no financial need, she still keeps her hands busy by making lace in the traditional way. This is her wedding present to you."

Chara turned to let Quentin drape the precious lace over her shoulders. "Will you thank your friend's grandmother for me?"

"I have, but you can also drop her a note, if you wish. I'll give you the address. I've arranged for your own monogrammed stationery to be delivered to you tomorrow."

Chara bit her lip to keep from telling him that at twenty-five she was fully aware of the proper courtesies toward a gift given.

The show at the Forty-sixth Street Theater was typical of the slick, sophisticated musicals that run on Broadway —the language was graphic and funny, the songs, toe tappers. A few times Chara found herself laughing so hard her side hurt. She realized that Quentin watched her more often than he did the show.

45

"I'm shocked that you don't find this too spicy, bride," he drawled in her ear.

"I heard worse when I was in college and much worse in our law firm." Chara bristled.

"Now I'm really shocked, Chara. I thought you had been protected by convent walls, then, later, by dusty tomes of the law."

"I don't know what my mother might have told you about me, but let me set you straight about one thing," she hissed, hearing the shushes around them. "I attended a first-rate fine arts college and our firm handled some of the most colorful cases in Los Angeles County. So don't mock me," she bit out, moving as far away from him as she could in the narrow theater seat.

"Am I doing that? I thought I was mocking myself."

At intermission Quentin introduced Chara to several people who stared at her with open curiosity. She thought some of the women's looks were downright malevolent. It was Chara's guess that the diminutive redhead named Rhea had been more than a friend to Quentin, but when the woman tried to ease herself between them, he pulled Chara close to his side. When she felt his lips at her nape she couldn't stop the redness from rising into her face.

After the intermission he seemed to ignore her, to Chara's relief, until the curtain came down and they were standing outside the theater. "We'll walk from here, Chara. The club I have in mind isn't far. Dominic's. Have you heard of it? No? Well, I'll enjoy showing it to you. You may see some of the people you met at intermission."

Chara didn't respond and they walked the several blocks in silence, other well-dressed persons strolling in the same direction.

The club was so dark that Chara had to stay close to Quentin or lose him. The maître d' laughed and joked with him before leaving them at a tiny booth. The music was rhythmic and exciting. Of its own accord, her toe began keeping time on the floor as she sipped the white wine Quentin had ordered for her.

"Come on, Chara. We'll dance," he whispered, leading her to the floor.

They danced apart at first, since the number was fast. Chara, who had always loved to dance, gave herself up completely to the music, swaying and gyrating in joyous abandon, knowing that Quentin's eyes were on her the entire time. Then the tempo changed and became sultry and the words to the love song they had danced to in Vegas were sobbed into the microphone, making Chara remember their time together vividly.

"Our song, I think," Quentin muttered, pulling her tight to him, both of his arms about her, one, low, curving her spine, the other, high, stroking her neck. It was so pleasurable, it made her weak, relaxing her against him, her own arms raising to entwine at his neck. Her fingers plucked lightly at the black, curling hair touching his collar. She felt a flood of happiness. Without thinking she began to hum the love song.

"Quite the enchantress, aren't you, bride?" Quentin queried, nibbling at her ear. "I think you're a chameleon, Chara. One moment you're a tiger, then you're a little girl, now you're a total Circe. Do you know how many men watched you and your uninhibited dancing? I know exactly," he murmured, his lips feathering her ear as he bent over her. "Sing the words to me, Chara. Please," Quentin husked, holding her lightly but very close.

For a moment Chara was going to refuse, but the pull of the song and Quentin's persuasive voice were too strong. She sang, hesitantly at first as she hunted for the words in her memory, then her voice deepened to the softness and richness of velvet, the words of love suddenly meaningful in her mind.

She wasn't sure how long they danced. Quentin seemed

47

reluctant to release her, urging her to sing other ballads into his ear.

A feeling of languor was stealing over Chara as between sips of chilled Chablis they danced and danced until it was very late. In the taxi, going home, Chara didn't move away when Quentin sat close to her, his arm pressing down the length of hers. When they alighted from the cab and were whisked up in the elevator, they remained silent, Chara's heart already doing double time at the thought of lying in Quentin's arms.

Unwilling to let him see how unnerved she was by him, Chara went straight to the lounge and the drink cabinet.

"Didn't you have enough to drink at the club, Chara?" Quentin drawled, touching his lighter to a cheroot, but not taking his eyes from her. To Chara he did look like Lucifer in the dancing flame of the lighter. He looked no less dangerous when the light was extinguished.

"I'm thirsty." Chara cleared her throat, hating the squeaky sound of her voice. "Would you like something?"

"Yes. You." His eyes fixed on her like a sonar beam, as though they were picking up messages from her face. "I'll wait while you drink the Perrier, Chara. Then I think it's time for bed."

"Maybe . . . maybe I'm not sleepy." She hedged, her heart fluttering like a trapped bird.

"Oh, I think you're ready for bed, Chara." Quent smiled, walking toward her, taking the glass from her hand, then lifting her into his arms. "You're very ready, bride."

She was both shocked and excited when he insisted on undressing her, not even bothering to turn down the lamp. When she stood naked to that hot silver gaze, it seemed the most natural thing in the world for her to undress Quentin. Before she was half through, Quentin had swung her up in his arms again. "You're headier than any alcohol, Chara."

48

She closed her eyes as she felt him sink beside her on the bed, her arms reaching up to hold him close, wishing she had the strength to deny him.

Chara sighed, letting her head fall against the cushioned back of the bucket seat of the deep green Jaguar.

"Tired? Bored?" Quent drawled, not taking his eyes from the thruway as he touched the lighter to his fragrant cheroot. He knew by now that Chara liked the aroma even though she didn't smoke herself.

"Not a bit bored," she stated, gazing at the passing scenery. "A little tired, yes. We did a great deal in two days."

"Didn't we though?" Quentin whispered, reaching out a hand to touch her thigh.

"I didn't mean . . ." Chara faltered, then stiffened as she heard his low laugh.

"I know what you meant, bride. I was just teasing. Tell me, Chara, who has the most profound philosophies? The cabbies or the waiters?"

Chara's soft laugh brought Quentin's head around in a quick, intense look. "Do you remember that waiter telling me I couldn't have cheesecake at two o'clock in the morning—" Chara's voice wobbled in amusement "—then bringing you a stein of beer and a corned beef sandwich because . . ."

"It would be better for me at that time of the morning," Quentin added. Chara burbled, liking Quentin's laugh when it joined hers. It was full and deep.

There were other moments they recalled and laughed over. It surprised Chara that she had genuinely enjoyed Quentin's companionship. She couldn't remember ever having two such carefree days as she had just had in New York City. She had never felt such happiness.

They drove through the Montezuma Swamps and Chara was thrilled when Quentin pointed out the beautiful hawks sweeping so low it seemed their wings would touch the car.

"But this isn't new for you, is it, Chara? You went to school around here," Quentin said.

"In Rochester. But I've never been down here and the only Finger Lake I've ever seen was Canandaigua Lake. This is beautiful," Chara said as they drove along the lovely, curving Route 89, which was the lake road on Cayuga's west side and the last twenty miles of their journey. "Why didn't we just drive from New York City to here instead of flying to Syracuse, Quent?"

"It's better than a six-hour drive and only about a forty-minute flight, that's why. Saves energy . . . mine. Look, Chara, there's the lake. We'll be home in twenty minutes. What do you say to a swim first, maybe a sail if the wind is right? Then maybe we'll lie on the beach, later barbecue a couple of steaks. All right?"

Chara nodded, craning her neck to see more of the lake. She was surprised at the size. Quentin informed her that Cayuga Lake was the second largest of the big Finger Lakes, forty-two miles long and about four miles wide at the widest part. Quentin explained that his place was about halfway down the lake.

Chara was not prepared for the modern, natural cedar, shingled ranch house that perched on the top of a knoll in the middle of vineyards overlooking a wide expanse of lake.

They hurried like two children, putting their bags in the bedrooms, then changing into swimsuits.

Chara laughed at the pink and white awning that was stretched over the jeep roll bar.

Quentin gave her a rueful grin. "Don't laugh at our jeep, Chara." He pointed over his head. "My niece's idea. You don't know the struggle I had to keep her from painting the whole thing pink." Quentin geared down as they descended the angled, steep dirt road leading to the beach.

50

"Here we are. Last one in gets to do clean-up after dinner . . ."

As Quentin said this he stopped the jeep with a jerk and jumped from his seat to the beach, stripping off his shirt as he ran. Before Chara could move, he was on the wide stone jetty, running to the end and springing from the diving board in a well-executed racing dive.

Is there anything that man doesn't do well? Chara grumbled to herself as she shook off her espadrilles and beach jacket. She was in the air in a modified swan dive before she remembered that she didn't have her Speedo suit on. Instead she had donned her blue polka-dot bikini. She felt the top give way underwater and tried frantically to grab for it. Coughing to rid herself of swallowed water, she surfaced empty-handed and topless. Quentin's grinning face was in front of her, the flimsy strip of cloth clutched in one fist. He was treading water and laughing.

"Lose something, bride? I must say you look very fetching."

"Give me that," Chara sputtered, trying not to laugh.

"New brides mustn't shout at their husbands, Chara," he admonished her, kicking away from her easily.

"Quent, stop fooling and give me my top."

"Say please . . . and pay the forfeit."

Chara treaded water, wary and suspicious, trying to keep well away from Quentin but sure he had a very good view of her breasts. "What forfeit?"

"One kiss," Quent drawled, his smile irritating her.

"All right," Chara agreed. "Give me the top and I'll pay."

"Say please, Chara."

"Please, you . . . you . . ."

"Tsk, tsk, no temper. Here, catch."

As Chara reached for the top, she looked away from Quentin to follow the descent of the material. She gasped as Quentin's strong arms enclosed her even as she snatched the suit. Her protest was smothered by his mouth. His kiss was thirst-quenching, much as a dry man takes water from a spring. She felt again the electric excitement as his tongue explored hers. She hardly struggled as the water closed over her head, knowing she wanted his stroking hand to remain at her breast.

She burst to the surface, choking for air. She swam back to the jetty and in its shadow she refastened the errant top. When she turned, Quentin was swimming far out in the lake with sure, strong strokes that were carrying him parallel to the beach. A wake creamed out behind him as he increased his speed. Chara had watched some of the Olympic contenders at Mission Viejo and she felt that Quentin could have held his own with most of them.

She swam back out into the lake, her easy crawl stroke carrying her into deeper water. She took care not to swim near Quentin.

Two young men she judged to be her age or a little older swept by in a Sunfish, hailing her and asking if she'd like a ride. She gave them a wide smile but shook her head no. Somehow she knew that Quentin wouldn't welcome the intrusion.

After floating and swimming awhile, she felt chilled. The water was much crisper and colder than the bathtub pools she had been using in southern California. As she swam closer to shore, she saw Quentin shampooing his head. Her look of inquiry was met with a laugh and quick toss of a plastic bottle in her direction.

"Try it. Everybody around here washes their hair in the lake. I guarantee you'll like the result."

Skeptical but game, Chara peeled off the bathing cap that had confined her long hair and began to soap her head. She was amazed at how little soap it took to create a mound of lather. She felt other hands on her head but didn't try to open her eyes.

"Come on, Chara. Swim out, then we'll dive down and rinse it."

By the time she and Quentin were ready to come out, Chara was laughing and shivering at the same time. On the jetty Quentin wrapped her in a bath sheet, then left her to start a fire on the beach. Even though the sun was shining brightly, the warmth of the fire was very welcome to the shivering Chara.

"A little early in the game to be picking up strangers, isn't it, Chara?" Quentin drawled, toweling himself dry on the other side of the fire.

Dragging her eyes away from his torso, Chara picked up a stone and skipped it toward the water. "Just what the hell do you mean by that?"

"Don't talk tough, Chara. I've told you I don't like it."

"And I've told you I don't care what you like."

"And you know damn well what I mean. Fooling around with summer Romeos."

"I wasn't fooling around. They asked if I would like a ride. I said no. If I had known you were going to be such a great big grouch daddy, I would have gone. You know what they say about being hanged for a sheep . . ." Chara said, her tones sweet.

The Arctic eyes hardened even more as they roved over her. "You have a sharp tongue for a little girl."

Chara could hardly take her eyes from Quentin as he sank down, his towel stretched next to hers. His flimsy black Lycra trunks barely covered him. The flexing of his chest and leg muscles as he lay back mesmerized her. Anger at herself made her lash out even more at Quentin.

"If this little girl annoys you, I can make an effort to keep her out of your way. I'm sure those boys in the sailboat would be happy to keep me amused, then you can run after those bigger girls you always seemed to have hanging around." Chara took a deep breath and turned on her back, not able to meet that silver-eyed stare. How she

53

hated the kind of man he was, Chara fumed to herself. She wasn't aware he had moved closer until she felt his breath feather her ear when he spoke. "Take a nap. Maybe you won't be so touchy when you waken."

Chara ignored him and closed her eyes.

Still half asleep, she reached up a lazy hand to swipe at the fly that was touching her cheek. Her hand encountered a lightly stubbled cheek. Her eyes open now, she studied Quentin, whose lips were still questing her cheek in feather-light kisses.

"I'm glad you don't snore, Chara, but you do sleep with your mouth open just a little, like this," Quentin whispered as his one hand touched her mouth, parting her lips a fraction. "You have lovely soft lips, Chara." He lowered his hand to her waist and scooped her under his body as his mouth touched hers. Chara was stunned by his gentleness. Just as her one hand came up to clasp him, Quentin rolled away from her and to his feet all in one fluid motion. He faced away from her, looking south down the lake. "That's Sheldrake Point down there, Chara." He spoke in a flat tone. "We'll go down in the boat one day." He pointed to the cliffs across the lake, saying that though she couldn't see them, there were quite a few cottages at the base of them. "That red spire a little to the north on the other side is Wells College, a very old girls' school founded by the Wells Fargo people. Remember the wagon trains that carried the gold in all those John Wayne movies."

Chara nodded, intrigued. Quentin was a fountain of information about the area. She listened closely as they strolled along the shale beach. He told her of the sacred Indian grounds that the Senecas were trying to reclaim, about the great chief Red Jacket who was considered to be one of the truly great peacemakers. He was also an outstanding war tactician when he had to be. Like the Greeks and the Romans, Indians of the Iroquios Nation prized elocution. In this department Red Jacket had no peer. Even the white men were impressed. He came to be one of the Iroquois Nation's greatest orators. Oratory was prized among the Iroquois, and those with such talent were considered to be blessed and very special, Quentin told her, his tones soft.

When Chara stumbled on a stone because she was trying to look at everything at once, Quentin took her hand, covering it with his own. Chara thought it odd that she should feel so at peace with a man she despised. As she watched two blue-mantled kingfishers diving at the shoreline for food, a gust of laughter broke from her.

"Listen to how angry they are with us," Chara exclaimed, swinging Quentin's hand with her own.

"Kingfishers are always like that. One of the toughest, most graceful birds you'll ever see. Look out there! Did you see that fish jump? Big fellow, whatever he was. Come on. We'll go back. Time to get the fire started. Are you hungry?"

"Starving. I'll make the salad. Race you back to the towels."

As Chara said this she broke away from Quentin, sprinting down the beach, trying to avoid the boulders and driftwood. It looked almost as though she would make it, when all at once Quentin stretched past her without straining, and Chara was sure he could have passed her at any time. She marveled again at his tall, dark, good looks and the great physical shape he kept himself in.

Later, after she had showered, Chara donned an aqua cotton sundress, the shirred strapless bodice emphasizing her rounded breasts. She twirled the full skirt to look in the mirror, satisfied that the color enhanced her eyes and gave her hair a deeper honey hue. Blue was her best color.

When she slid back the screen door leading to the patio, Quentin turned from the gas grill where he was monitoring two steaks to look at her. "You look like a very sophisticated eighteen, not the twenty-six you'll be two weeks from now. I like to see you dressed like that, Cinderella. Are those heels a little high for you?"

"No. Do you like them?" she demanded, suddenly wanting his admiring glance to stay on her, a little breathless as those silver eyes dropped again to her legs.

"I like the effect very much. You have delightful legs, little bride, as I'm sure you are quite aware. You look like a blueberry ice cream cone . . . good enough to eat," Quent declared as he handed Chara a tall frosty drink with a twist of lime in it. "Tonic and lime with just a touch of vodka. It pleases me that you're not much of a drinker. Booze has a way of aging a woman."

"Men too, I think," Chara responded tartly, clinking her glass against his, then taking a sip of the icy liquid, her tongue coming out to catch an errant drop. When she saw Quentin's gaze on her mouth, she turned away, confused by her feelings toward him. She felt alive. She felt her skin quiver and move. She felt daring and reckless. She admonished herself, trying to keep herself on keel. Chara watched Quentin through the curtain of her lashes, feeling an almost irresistible urge to prod him, goad him, make him angry—anything as long as he touched her with those long, capable hands.

Some of the drink sloshed over the side of her glass, spilling on her. She felt Quentin train those all-seeing eyes on her, and under cover of wiping up the spill, she didn't look at him. She felt X-rayed by his intent gaze. She set her glass down on a glass-topped table, careful to keep her eyes averted.

A large bowl of spinach, washed and stripped, sat in a larger bowl of ice, a side tray of fixings nearby. An array of bottles of vinegar, oil, and various condiments sat on another tray. Glad of something to do, Chara bent to her task. Edging the salad with hard-cooked eggs, she then sprinkled crumbled bacon bits over it. Covertly she watched Quentin when she finished the salad, admiring the cream-colored denims and matching silk shirt that clung to his broad-shouldered, narrow-hipped build.

"How tall are you, Quent?" she queried, feeling a little breathless.

Quentin straightened away from the grill, the long-handled tongs gripped in his right hand, his narrow-eyed glance seeming to reach out and touch her. "I'm six foot three. Why do you ask, Chara?"

Chara looked away from him, shrugging, feeling her cheeks redden. "I just wondered. I'm tall myself. Usually when I wear heels I'm as tall as most, taller than some." she answered, her voice a little husky.

Quentin spoke right behind her, his one arm curving around her waist to pull her back against him. "With me you're just right, little bride. With those heels on, you come right to my chin," he whispered, turning her in his arms, his mouth coming down and brushing hers lightly before it pressed hard and punishing. "Sit down, Chara. The steaks are done." His eyes missed nothing, his smile made her shiver.

They spoke little during dinner, but Chara could feel Quentin watching her. When she passed her wineglass to be refilled, she avoided eye contact with that hard gaze. He paused long seconds before he filled her glass. By the time they had reached the Brie and fresh fruit, Chara was feeling a little woozy. Just to escape his gimlet stare, she cleared the dirty dishes and carried them through to the oak-paneled kitchen. She slid her feet experimentally across the smooth terrazzo floor, giggling as she staggered, a cup rattling against the plate. She hadn't realized Quentin had followed her until he spoke.

"Little girls should drink milk if they have reached the age of twenty-six and still can't hold their alcohol," he said at her shoulder. "I don't like women who make fools of themselves."

The anger in his voice ignited her own temper. "I've told you before, I'm not one of your . . . your women. I'm not the type, remember! And . . . and even . . . oops." Chara hiccuped. "Excuse me. What was I saying? Oh, yes, even if I were your type, I still wouldn't let you tell me what to do, Mr. Wonderful Wainwright."

"I'm warning you, Chara, behave yourself," Quentin hissed.

Chara flipped her hand under her chin in an Italian gesture she had learned from one of her fellow paralegals, Maria Donti, who was a first-generation American. Chara knew it was rude, but that was how she felt toward Quentin at the moment.

"Chara, damn you, behave like a lady," he snarled.

Chara dumped the plates on the counter and turned to look at him, her temperature at full boil. "Drop dead," she countered. "By the way, Big Daddy, what kind of fun and games have you planned for us tonight?"

The cold lightning in Quentin's eyes made Chara press back against the counter. "I'm not Captain Kangaroo, brat. Why don't you find yourself a comic book and read it. That should be just about the right intellectual level for you tonight." He flung this at her, then turned to the door. He paused and spoke without turning his head. "I won't be in until late. Don't forget to turn off the TV when you go to bed, little girl."

The slamming of the outside door jerked Chara from her daze. Impotent anger seized her and she picked up the thing nearest at hand, one of the bone china cups they had used for coffee. She threw it as hard as she could against the paneled wall, shattering it into a million pieces.

Even after cleaning up the mess and loading the dishwasher, she was still so angry she could have spat bullets. To add to the flame, the large amount of wine she drank was giving her a headache. Rubbing her hand across her forehead, she sighed. Maybe exercise would take the pain away. She donned her other bikini and grabbed a towel and went into the garage, where she took a flashlight from a shelf and backed out the jeep. Without too much trouble she drove it down the steep, winding dirt road to the beach. She was tempted to keep the headlights on when she arrived at the dark shale shingle, but fear of a dead battery decided her to use the flashlight instead. Stripping off her jeans and shirt, she placed the flashlight at the end of the pier and climbed down the ladder. The water made her gasp, but long hard strokes paralleling the beach soon warmed her. By the time she emerged she was cold, but her headache had lessened and she felt far more relaxed. Her anger had also cooled. She wondered how soon Quentin would get around to talking about a separation. She was confused by the stab of pain she felt at the thought. *Pull yourself together, Chara,* she chided herself, *soon you'll be back in L.A. doing the work you like with the kind of people you enjoy.* For some reason the thought didn't buoy her spirits.

As she towel-dried her hair, her mind kept going back to Quentin. She had never felt such tearing anger at another human being, yet she could relax with him. Her senses were sharper when she was with him. The rain steaming the pavements of New York City was fresher when she was running through it, her hand clasped tight in Quentin's. The songbirds in the trees above the beach seemed to have bell-clear tones when she had stood quietly with Quentin, his arm loose at her waist.

All at once Chara heard a scuffling sound and stiffened. Alarmed, realizing she was alone and isolated, she gripped the flashlight, swinging it in a wide arc. The first sweep of light showed her nothing, but Chara kept inching toward the jeep, clutching her towel to her like a shield. The second sweep of light caught a movement in the brush close to the cliff. She was about to turn and run when she heard the whining. "My God, it's a dog, a big dog," Chara muttered to herself, taking a cautious step toward the distressed animal. All the stories she had heard about being hurt by wounded animals crowded her mind.

When she leaned toward him, she saw that the animal was on his side, panting. Chara gasped when the gleam of the flash showed a trap biting into the leg of the dog.

"Oh, Lord, fellow, I don't know how to get you free," Chara moaned, trying to soothe the big creature by patting its head.

The shout from the water startled her to her feet.

"Hey, you with the flashlight, do you happen to know the blonde who was on this beach today?"

"I am the blonde who was on this beach today," Chara called.

"Hey, that's great. We're the guys that were in the sailboat. Would you like to go sail—"

"Please, could you tie up your motorboat and come here. I need some help," she interrupted, her voice tremulous and urgent.

Chara could hear scrambling around, then a bump as the boat was nosed into the jetty. She saw the running lights go out, then there was the sound of stumbling feet along the jetty. Chara lifted the light to guide them to her position.

"What the hell . . . ? Is this your dog? Oh, by the way, I'm Mark Jeffers and this is Brian Tarr. What happened?" the one in cut-off jeans asked.

"Hi, I'm Chara Styl . . . Wainwright. No, it isn't my dog and I don't know how that trap was put there, but he's in pain and we have to help him." Chara's voice shook as she looked at the anguished dog.

The boy called Brian told Chara to wrap her head scarf around the dog's muzzle. "Just as a protection from bite," he said. As Chara stayed at the head of the dog and tried to soothe it, the boys tried myriad ways of prying the teeth of the trap apart but to no avail. Chara was sure the dog was in agony. All at once she remembered the workbench in the garage and the large assortment of tools hanging there.

"Listen, could you help me get him into the jeep? Maybe if we got him up to the house . . . we could find a tool there that . . . would free poor Gulliver." Chara urged, sobs interrupting her words.

"I thought he wasn't your dog, but still you give him a name. Okay, okay, don't get mad. We'll hurry. Don't look so worried, we'll come with you." Mark patted the dog on the head. "You'll be all right, won't you, Gulliver?"

The ride to the house took forever, it seemed to Chara. She was in the back of the jeep with the dog and Brian was driving. Mark was turned around in the seat trying to soothe both Chara and the dog.

After working what seemed like hours, Chara had almost given up on freeing the dog from the teeth of the trap. Brian, who was searching around on the workbench in the garage, had found a crowbar. With great effort they were able to pry the trap open enough for Chara to ease the paw free. Even though they had retied the scarf around the dog's mouth, she heard it groan in pain.

Brian gave a yelp of discovery as he pulled something from the wall of the garage. "Hey, look at this, a first-aid box. Get some soapy water, Chara. Dishwashing liquid is good; it's strong."

The three of them were wholly absorbed in the task of cleaning the animal. When they were through, they sat back, each with a can of beer, and watched the big, black dog lap up a bowl of milk and cornflakes. Relieved at the results of their efforts, they laughed and joked every time the dog's tail thumped the cement floor.

In keeping with the festive mood, Chara went to get three more cold beers and brought with her a large bag of pretzels from the pantry. Mark tried to imitate Gulliver's

61

solemn munch that both chewed and swallowed in one motion.

Chara was sure she had not laughed so hard since her college floor parties. To Chara her college years and the one year she had studied in London had been the happiest and most carefree of her life. She had not once missed her mother or father when she had been at school. She had only missed Ken, whom she considered to be her only close family. She was laughing at something when she heard the angry roar.

"What the hell is going on here?" Quentin grated, looking much like a boxer coming out of his corner as he stood framed in the doorway.

Chara scrambled to her feet, spilling a little beer from the can on her chest. She swiped at the dribble traveling over her bare tummy, aware of Quentin's eyes raking over her. For all the time she had spent with Brian and Mark, who were close in age to Ken, dressed in her tiny bikini, she had felt no embarrassment. Now, feeling herself redden under the gaze of her husband, she tried to drape a towel around herself. She had to clear her throat twice before she could speak. "This is Mark and this is Brian. They were helping me with the dog." she explained, her voice husky.

"Oh?" Quentin snarled, looking the two young men over from head to toe.

"Yes," Chara defended, feeling protective toward the squirming young men. "And you needn't look like that, Quent. I found the dog—"

Mark stood, interrupting Chara, brushing his hands down the sides of his jeans, then putting his right one out toward Quentin. "That's right, sir. Your daughter was having difficulty—"

"Chara is my wife," Quentin growled. "Yes, you heard me right. She's my wife and not the teen-ager she appears to be. Now that I'm here, I think that I can take care of things. Good night . . . and . . . thanks." Quentin bit off the words, a muscle moving in his jaw. He had ignored Mark's proferred hand.

The two young men darted unbelieving looks at Chara that caused her to redden even more. Taking a deep breath, she followed the two of them out of the garage, avoiding Quentin's metallic stare.

"I'm . . . I'm sorry about that." She licked her lips. "I want you to know that I really appreciate what you did for Gulliver."

Mark cleared his throat. "That's all right, Chara. Hey, that's a pretty name. Do you spell it K-a-r-a?"

"No." Chara smiled, wishing that she could put them at their ease. "My father was a Greek scholar, among other things, so I was given a Greek name—C-h-a-r-a. Thank you again for what you did. Perhaps I'll see you again sometime," Chara said, not believing it to be true. She felt disappointment as she watched them turn away after they assured her that they wouldn't need a ride to the beach. She had enjoyed their company, relaxed in it. She sighed in regret.

She braced herself to face Quentin when she returned to the garage. Instead of an angry Quentin in a boxer's stance, she found him kneeling next to the resting dog, patting it and talking to it in soft tones. She cleared her throat.

"Don't worry, Chara, I'm not going to bite you. Just don't plan on encouraging those two . . ." he began.

"I wasn't encouraging them," Chara snapped. "I asked them for help. They gave it. They also happen to be my brother's age."

Quentin turned, balancing on his haunches, his eyes dissecting Chara. "But you look their age . . . or younger," he grated, then forestalled the angry retort he could see building in her by saying, "Let's drop the subject, Chara.

Just remember I don't want you swimming alone. If you wish to swim at night, I'll go with you."

"You weren't here. What am I supposed to do? Wait until you have the time or inclination to accompany me?" Chara spat at him, not caring that his eyes had that liquid silver look that told her that his temper was not far below the surface.

"Just remember what I said. Now go to bed. I'll be along in a moment. The dog . . ."

"Gulliver. Call him Gulliver. That's his name." She gulped, willing the tears not to spill from her eyes.

"All right. Gulliver can sleep here in the garage, but you do understand that a dog like this no doubt belongs to someone. I don't think he's a purebred. He's large even for a Labrador. Just the same, someone probably keeps him for hunting, so don't set your heart on having him. I'll call an ad in to the local paper tomorrow."

Chara turned away without answering and rushed from the garage to the bathroom as though demons were after her. She let the cold spray of the shower pummel her overheated skin until she calmed down somewhat. "Damn the man," she muttered to herself as she dried herself, "someday I'm going to drop him over the cliff."

As much as she told herself she wouldn't let him make love to her that night, when he came to her he seemed to sense how she felt and teased her in a gentle, persuasive way that destroyed all her defenses. In moments she was clinging to him, urging him to love her, trying her best to arouse him as he was arousing her. The gentleness became a storm.

Sleep didn't come even though Chara was tired. She was able to move out of Quentin's arms after a while when his breathing deepened. Their lovemaking had seemed to become more violent, more of a rampage, as though neither one could control the overflow of emotion. Chara had come to bed fully prepared to refuse Quentin, to repel every advance, but as usual his determined if gentle stroking had soon reduced her to jelly, making her respond when she didn't want to do so, finally even making her the impatient, aggressive one, urging him to love her so that their final coming together was like an explosion. She squirmed when she thought of it.

She had willed herself to sleep to no avail. When Gulliver began to whine about two o'clock in the morning, she was still wide awake. She eased herself from the bed in as quiet a fashion as she could manage, not wanting to waken Quentin. From the bedside table she took the small travel alarm clock that had been with her since college and rummaged until she found an old sweat jacket that she had used for years for jogging.

The dog was very glad to see her. When Chara felt his nose, it was hot and dry. She washed the leg again very carefully, crooning to him the whole time. Then she rebandaged it and went back into the house for some ice cold milk to put in his dish.

The kitchen light flashing on blinded her for a moment and the dish of milk rocked in her hands and some spilled over the side. "Now look what you've done, Quent! You've made me spill the milk. Must you always creep up on people?" Chara asked, her voice querulous, her teeth biting at her lower lip. She stared at the short terry wrap around Quentin's hips and knew he was naked underneath.

He read her irritated look with mocking eyes. "Now don't start ripping up at me about this." He laughed at her. "You know I never wear pajamas. You should be glad I've made the concession to this," he drawled, his hand swiping at the hip-hugging maroon wrap. "What are you doing up at this hour? I awoke and you were gone. I didn't like it."

"Gulliver has a slight fever and he's quite lonely. I

wanted to give him some milk," Chara mumbled, quite giddy at his words, sensing he was following her when she left the kitchen.

"Chara, for God's sake . . . what is that?" he barked, laughing. "An alarm clock? That's only for puppies, as I understand it. Isn't that your jacket he's cuddled up to?" he quizzed, his eyes narrowed, as she lifted her chin.

Stepping to Chara's side, Quentin took the milk from her hands and set it down in front of the dog, then straightened, taking her chin in his hand. "Now don't start getting feisty with me at two thirty in the morning. Smile," he demanded, his fingers gripping her chin. "Smile for me, Chara. It shouldn't be too hard." The smile was all at once harsh. "You had no trouble laughing it up with those boys." The silver eyes turned into concrete.

For a fleeting moment Chara wondered if he could be jealous, but then she chided herself for imagining that flicker deep in his eyes. She jerked her chin away from his fingers, looking down at the now contented, drowsy dog as she spoke. "Perhaps I would laugh and smile more if you didn't act like my warden. I just don't . . ." Chara's voice trailed off as she heard his indrawn breath.

"Warden, am I?" he rasped, one arm reaching out for her, dragging her to his bare chest. She pushed at him, opening her mouth to protest, even as his was coming down to meet hers. The shock of intimate contact rendered her motionless as his mouth plundered hers, his tongue gentle and probing. Her body felt like a melting candle; her hands reached up in tentative search around the strong column of his neck. She pulled at the short hairs there and heard him gasp as her fingers threaded tighter. It gave her a feeling of power to feel his heart pounding against her own. Excited by his hardening body against hers, she pressed closer, liking the feathering of ragged breath as his lips traveled to her cheeks, then to her eyes, then downward to her throat. She felt herself lifted higher

66

by his arms until her toes were dangling above the garage floor. She clung tighter as Quentin's mouth seared her skin. She gasped as her nipples hardened under his onslaught. She closed her eyes, wanting the sensation to go on forever, knowing she had never been alive until Quentin had come into her life.

At Gulliver's rumbling growl Quentin lifted his head, not releasing Chara. "Easy, boy. I'm not hurting your lady." Quentin's laugh was a little shaky as he let Chara slide down his body, pressing a quick kiss in her hair. "He's worried, Chara. He's not sure that what we were doing is friendly."

"I'm not sure about that myself," Chara whispered, pulling free from Quentin and kneeling in front of the dog. "There, there, Gulliver. Everything's fine. Go to sleep." Chara soothed him. Then standing, she motioned to Quentin, taking the time to tuck the clock closer as she bent over the dog again. She and Quentin said nothing until they reached the kitchen. "Would you like a drink of something?" Chara asked, not looking at him. When he murmured "yes," she opened the refrigerator. "Milk all right? Or would you like lemonade?" she queried, feeling uncomfortable because she knew he was staring at her.

"Milk is fine, Chara," he said. "What's wrong, Chara? Surely you're not embarrassed because of our lovemaking in the garage, are you?"

"Lovemaking? Was that what it was? I thought it was lust making," she thrust at him, wanting to pierce that armor of his. "Here's your milk." She banged the glass down on the counter. "I'm not thirsty." She stormed away from him, and out of the kitchen, down the hall to the bedroom. "What's the matter with me?" she moaned to herself, her face pressed into the pillow on the bed. "Why do I attack him?"

When Quentin came to bed, he said nothing but turned on his side away from her. For the first night since their first night together, Chara didn't fall asleep held tight in Quentin's arms. She lay there wide awake and miserable long after Quentin was asleep.

Deep in sleep, she didn't awaken until sunlight filtered through the sheer drapes and nudged her eyes open. She watched as Quentin started to leave the bedroom dressed in jeans. He had just left a tall iced orange juice on the bedside table. "Thank you, but you don't have to wait on me," Chara husked.

Quentin spoke without turning around, his voice cold. "I had an ulterior motive. There's a good breeze out on the lake. You had said you would like to go sailing. If you want to go with me, you had better drink that juice and get ready." His tones were clipped and he still hadn't turned to look at her. "I have a flask of coffee for the boat. If you want to go, hurry. If not, just say so," he finished.

With a sinking feeling Chara realized he just didn't care if she went or not. Wanting to tell him to go to hell warred with an urgent wish not to be left behind alone. The thought of sailing on that crystal lake catapulted her out of bed. "I'm coming," she said as she sprinted for the bathroom. She showered and dressed in minutes.

Only slightly flushed from hurrying, she detoured through the kitchen, snatching two peaches and two oranges before she joined Quentin in the jeep.

Coloring as she watched him run his eyes over her, she wished for a moment she hadn't donned the faded cut-off jeans that fitted like a too tight glove over her rounded behind. The jeans were frayed and worn thin in the seat. She had had them since college and could never bear to part with them. She had tied a paint-daubed shirt, which she had used when painting her apartment in L.A. and which was almost as dear to her as the jeans, under her breasts. To complete her outfit she had twisted her hair into a topknot which she had covered with a beat-up sailor hat, brim down. She fidgeted under Quentin's stare as she climbed into the jeep, then, her chin at a defiant angle, she turned to face him on the seat. "I thought you said to hurry, so I did. You don't wear good clothes sailing, you know."

"No, you don't," Quentin answered, a reluctant smile touching his mouth. "You look ten years old, Chara. I'll have to start making you carry your birth certificate with you. I might get picked up for contributing to the delinquency of a minor."

"Serve you right," Chara snapped, a dizzy happiness filling her because Quentin wasn't angry with her anymore.

From the minute the wind caught in the Sunfish's sail and they raced over the water, Chara felt free and unfettered; her laughter carried high into the sparkling breeze. Eyes sparkling, she obeyed Quentin when he told her to scull out, their bodies almost paralleling the water. The silence, the speed, the crying gulls all contributed to Chara's mounting exhilaration.

"Are you happy, Chara?" Quentin asked as they came about and Chara squealed as the boat rocked.

"Yes, yes, this is exciting." Chara laughed openmouthed when Quentin insisted that she take the tiller and handle the sheets. The small uncomplicated craft was easy to maneuver, and before long Chara was confident of her handling of it. Quentin gave her deft, terse instruction, not turning a hair when they heeled over so much Chara was sure they would go over. "Don't worry about turning over, Chara. A Sunfish can be righted easily."

It was a fairly long sail to the island, so Chara had a chance to see many of the cottages along the shore. She waved to all the other boats that passed near them. It was a beautiful day and Quentin was smiling at her.

When they neared the island, Chara watched as Quentin backed the boat, then lifted her out.

"This island was and is sacred to the Indians," Quent

69

whispered in her ear, his arm resting at her waist to help her over the stones. They circled the small island in virtual silence, the screeching gulls overhead the only disturbance, then sat down not too far from the boat. Chara peeled one of the oranges she had brought with her, placing the peel back into the bag. She was about to hand one wedge to Quentin when he leaned back on his elbows and opened his mouth. Smiling, she placed it between his lips. Then he leaned on one elbow and took a wedge from her and pressed it between her teeth. Laughing, Chara bit down and the juice squirted onto Quentin.

"Was that on purpose?" he growled, a gleam in his eye.

Chara shook her head, still laughing as she peeled the other orange. Again Quentin opened his mouth and took the wedge of orange from her. Repeating her part, she took one from him, enjoying the game because they were not at odds with one another. This time when she bit down on the orange, it was hard, insuring that it would squirt. It caught Quentin in the face and Chara couldn't control her mirth. She tried to back away from his reaching hands, but he pulled her down on top of himself until their faces were just inches apart.

"That was no accident." Quentin breathed against her face, his hands making exciting patterns on the bare skin of her back as he rubbed her midriff.

"Yes, yes, it was." Chara laughed, all at once breathless as she felt the familiar languor steal over her at his touch. She tried to press back from him, but his arms were steel bands holding her in place. "Quent, someone might come by in a boat."

"Little girls have to be punished," Quentin muttered, his voice a little thick.

"I'm not a little girl. I'm a twenty-five-year-old married lady." She choked, still laughing as she struggled against him.

"You look too much like a little girl," Quentin growled. "And I don't know whether I like it . . . or hate it."

Chara stared down into Quentin's pewter eyes, seeing the flicker of violence in their depths. Before she could fully comprehend what his eyes were telling her, the look was gone and she was sure she had imagined the message she saw there. With one easy motion, he swung her over until she was beneath him, the sailor hat falling backward to the ground. Imprisoning her with his body, he brought one hand up to loosen her topknot.

"I like your hair free, Chara. You can tie it up again when we get back in the boat." His hands threaded through her hair like a wide-toothed comb, sending shivers through her body. The languid feeling she fought so hard against when they were together was veining through her. A fleeting resentment touched her at the magnetic hold he had over her, at her inability to combat it no matter how hard she tried. Would she be able to break the grip he had on her once he had tired of her, she questioned herself, not liking the thoughts that crowded her mind at the question. What type of woman would follow her in Quentin's life? She wouldn't be so outspoken, Chara was sure. A darkly exotic woman walked through her mind, Latin and sensual. Come-hither brown eyes would make Quentin forget that he once professed to love blue ones. Maybe a tall auburn-haired beauty with slanting green eyes and a throaty laugh who would move like silk and make Quentin wonder what he ever saw in a blonde who was so stupid that she had remained a virgin until she was twenty-five and then had trapped him into marriage. Chara could see the redhead whispering to Quentin, telling him to shuck the dumb blonde like a snake shucks its skin. Inwardly Chara writhed as she watched Quentin laugh with the redhead, then kiss the Latin beauty; then he was surrounded by raving women who were straining to get near him, shouldering Chara aside.

"Chara? Chara, what are you thinking? You're a million miles away," Quentin husked, feathering her neck with tiny kisses.

Blinking, Chara looked down at him, not realizing her eyes had a pained, haunted look. "I . . . I was just day-dreaming."

Quentin fastened his teeth on her earlobe, sending shock waves of pleasure coursing through her. "Were you worried about Gulliver? Is that why you had that lovely mouth curved downward? You mustn't worry about it, love. Everything will work out fine. You'll see. Umm, you have the most delicious mouth, Chara. Let me have a taste."

Gasping, Chara felt his nibble on her lip, in awe at the ripples of pleasure running through her. "Quent . . . when you do that . . . it makes me feel . . . so . . . so . . ."

"Tell me, love, how do you feel. If you feel anything like I do, you feel like a volcano in full spate."

Before she could frame an answer, he let his mouth wander to her eyes, covering them with kisses, freezing her words in her throat. Her own hands had a life of their own, lifting to his cheeks, loving the feel of his smooth-shaven face.

"Chara," he groaned, lowering himself on her. She closed her eyes, but it seemed to her she could see the gull crying over her head, even behind her closed lids. Every tone of its speechlike cry was crystal clear to her sharpened ears, each sense magnified in the heat and wonder of her feelings. Her sky and sea and land was Quentin's body pressing into hers, his mouth was food and drink. She reveled in the floating sensation that invaded her body.

Quentin's questing hands untied her denim shirt, releasing her breasts to his hands. "Chara, my love, you have gorgeous breasts."

Sighing, she relaxed against him, letting her parted lips caress his jawline. When he brought his mouth back to hers, the stabbing motion of his tongue heated her to fever pitch, her own tongue teasing him back. She felt the shudder go through his body as he clamped her more tightly to him, sliding his one hand along her thigh. Chara wriggled with pleasure and felt his heart under her hands accelerate even more. His mouth left hers to slide over her cheek, kissing the skin under her ear. She felt as though she were falling and clung to his neck as he took first one breast with his mouth and then the other. Through a haze Chara realized that Quentin was breathing as though he were suffocating.

"Chara, I can't stop wanting you," he groaned.

All at once the derisive hoot of a power-boat horn drove them apart, sending a scowling Quentin to his feet. The jerky motion of his hand as he swiped at his hair told Chara more than his pallor that he wasn't in control of himself. "Damn it, Chara, cover yourself," Quentin rasped, then strode toward the other side of the island.

Confused and more than a little embarrassed by his attitude, her hands fumbled with the tails of her shirt. Why blame her if a boat happened to come by, Chara seethed, bending to gather the scattered orange peel that had fallen from the bag. What right did he have to fly into a rage because someone tooted at them? She would never understand his mercurial personality.

By the time Quentin returned, Chara was sitting cross-legged on the beach, her hat in place, her shirt tied, ready to leave. She glared at the sheen of water on his hair that told her he had been swimming. "I thought you told me not to swim alone. Doesn't that hold true for you as well?" she asked, her voice haughty. "But then I suppose you're such a jock, nothing could happen to you, right?"

"Don't be a shrew, Chara. It isn't attractive."

"Me, a shrew?" Chara yelped. "What do you call yourself then? You . . . you nasty-tempered crab. All you do is blow hot and cold. One minute you're smiling, the next you're shouting at me as though I were a criminal or something." Chara jumped to her feet, facing him, arms akimbo. "Why don't you tell me to leave if you despise me so much. I'll be glad to go." Chara lied. "I don't understand you. I never will."

Quentin looked at her narrow-eyed. "You'd like that, wouldn't you? If I asked you to go? Forget it Chara. You're staying with me whether you like it or not."

"I don't like it," Chara answered waspishly.

His head snapped back as though he had been hit. Chara took a step backward at the sudden look of violence in his eyes, a shuttered look coming over his face almost at once. "As I have said before, you have a sharp tongue. Get in the boat. We'll try to catch a fast wind back."

Chara lifted a shaky hand to her mouth, pushing by him and clambering into the Sunfish, trying to fight the urge to cry. Why couldn't they get along for even short periods without harsh words? It could have been such a wonderful day. She would need such moments to treasure up for the long arid days when she would be without Quentin. Just thinking of their intense lovemaking minutes ago was enough to throw her into turmoil. It made her body limp. She felt as though she had had a scorching sunburn from the inside out. She felt queasy, her limbs weakened. Angrily Chara looked at Quentin, his lazy, relaxed attitude at the tiller, his narrow-eyed gaze on the sail. He felt none of her tumult. He was an icy man, she grated to herself. To him it was all a game, she flagellated herself. Didn't he know that she had never considered falling in love because the battleground her parents had called marriage had left its ineradicable scars? How could he remain so untouched by the love that was wracking her?

Love . . . Chara straightened, in shock, from her sculling position, almost upsetting them. At Quentin's glare she resumed her position, her eyes not meeting his.

CHAPTER THREE

When they returned to the house, the phone was ringing but Chara didn't bother to answer it. Instead she stalked straight to the bedroom, feeling herself incapable of dealing with anything or anyone at the moment. Knowing she loved Quentin was a deep, tearing wound. She was bleeding to death inside and didn't know how to stop the flow. She threw herself across the bed, pushing her face into the pillows, trying to find someplace to hide. *You're stupid, Chara Wainwright, stupid.* She cursed herself for her weakness. *There's a cure,* she told her stupid self. *Slice him up in little pieces and barbecue him on the grill. No,* she yowled at her smart self, *I can't do that. I can't hurt him. Well, you had better hurt him,* the smart self argued back, *because if he ever finds out you love him, he'll laugh you right off the planet, stupid.*

She was still arguing with herself when she fell asleep, wondering in a fuzzy-minded way where all the fevered imagination had come from. Before she had met Quentin she had considered herself a pragmatic realist who was able to deal with the vagaries of life with coolness and dispatch. Now she had all the down-to-earth attitude of

Alice Through the Looking Glass. Chara promised herself she would learn how to fly and then become a Kamikaze pilot. On this comforting thought, she fell into a deep, dreamless sleep.

She awakened hungry and aware that there was someone sitting on the bed.

"Chara? Chara, come on. I know you're awake," Quentin said, his tones curt, his hand on the small of her back.

"You know that, do you? Well, that's more than I know," Chara muttered into her pillow, loath to turn over for fear that he'd take his hand away. She looked a little sideways under her upstretched arm, not able to see his face. Chara tensed when she felt his hand at her hip, his fingers touching her buttocks as though he couldn't help himself. Then he was pulling her over onto her back.

"What I'm trying to tell you is I've had a phone call about Gulliver." He smiled at her body stiffening under his hand. "Now don't look so worried. That was my sister Clem calling, saying that she thought the dog belonged to some campers. She checked around with some friends. It seems the dog did belong to the people my niece Amy had in mind, but it also seems that the people are no longer in the area and no one has heard of any inquiries about the dog. It looks as though if the dog is lost, the people are not too upset or they have deliberately abandoned him. Clem is of the opinion that with the high price of food, a dog of Gulliver's size is too expensive to feed." Quentin shrugged, spreading his hand in an upward who-knows gesture.

Chara levered herself into a sitting position, pushing her hair back with one hand, not taking her eyes from Quentin. "So do we keep him?" She swallowed hopefully.

Quentin's smile made her breath catch in her throat. "Let's just say we have a star boarder for the time being. If the people do come back to claim him, then we have to give him up, Chara."

76

"But . . . but until then, we can keep him. He's ours, isn't he, Quent?" Chara husked, not able to explain that she and Ken had never been allowed to have a pet of any kind, that her mother and father had considered anything that didn't concern themselves of no possible use whatsoever, that even after they had been divorced, neither parent was inclined to notice the need that children starved for love would have for an animal. Chara could still remember the tiny kitten that she and Ken had brought home so carefully, grateful that the housekeeper had provided them with milk and an old towel to make into a bed. The tearing grief that she and Ken had both felt when they had woken the next morning to find the kitty dispatched to the pound was still a bitter memory to Chara.

"What is it, Chara? You've gone off into one of your blue dreams again. Care to tell me about it?" Quentin's probing silver gaze seemed to touch each part of her face, his own features expressionless.

"It's just that . . . well . . . I . . . we . . . Ken and I never had a pet. I mean, I know that doesn't mean much, but, well, Gulliver is special, I guess," Chara explained, her eyes not quite meeting Quentin's.

"I see," Quentin said, his voice gentle, giving Chara the feeling that he did see, see all that she was unable to say to him. "Oh, one other thing, wife. My sister has invited us to dine with them tonight. I think we should go, but if you don't want to go, I'll call and make our excuses."

Chara's first feeling was that she didn't want to go. She didn't want to be put under the microscopic scrutiny of his family. She was sure she would be uncomfortable with anyone related to Quentin anyway. His hard stare made her hesitate before she answered. "Do they live far from here?" she equivocated, her fingers trembling on the peach silk bedspread. Chara all at once realized she was sitting on and had been sleeping on that elegant cover with her sailing clothes and sneakers. She scampered off on the

77

opposite side to where Quentin was sitting. She felt herself flush and cursed her inability to control it. *He'll think I'm acting like a gauche teen-ager,* she fumed to herself, watching his derisive smile. His sudden grin told her he had read her mind.

"No, Chara, to answer your question. They don't live far from here. Actually their house is just down the hill," Quentin said, his amusement growing as he watched her discomfort. "And, Chara, it's all right for you to do anything you choose in this house. After all, even if you do look like an adolescent, you are the lady of the house now, aren't you?"

She glared at him, grinding her teeth at the lopsided smile that made her pulse race. That decided her. She couldn't bear to be with him alone tonight after discovering that she loved him. She would act all wrong. She would do something to give herself away. The thought of Quentin finding out that she loved him horrified her. At that moment she wanted nothing more than to brain him with the table lamp and wipe that all-knowing grin from his face. "I've decided that I would like to go to your sister's house for dinner. What should I wear?"

Quentin shrugged. "It will be casual, so suit yourself. Besides, if I told you that I preferred you to wear slacks or jeans, you'd show up in a ball gown."

"How did you ever guess?" Chara asked sweetly.

"Just a wild stab, honey lamb," Quentin returned just as sweetly. He rose from the bed, walking to the door. In the opening he turned. "I thought I had better take Gulliver to the vet's in town. Would you like to come?"

Surprised, Chara smiled her pleasure, causing his eyes to flicker in that funny, arrested look that puzzled Chara. "That's a good idea, Quent. Thank you and yes I'd like to come . . . very much."

"Good. We'll leave after lunch. We will have to stop at the market and get more food for him as well. God, he eats like there's no tomorrow," Quentin ventured, his tones wry.

Chara nodded her head in agreement, laughing. When Quentin grinned at her again, she caught her breath. No wonder the women fall all over him, Chara mused. He's better looking than most of those sex symbols he directs on the screen.

Closing the door behind him, Chara began to strip off her clothing as she walked toward the bathroom. She sidestepped the sunken tub, looking at its cool tile depths longingly. She sighed as she stepped into the separate shower stall.

Forgetting herself in the invigorating needles of spray, she kept turning and twisting, rubbing herself with the loofah and the fragrant soap she always found there. Relaxed, she decided to shampoo her hair, not even trying to wipe the soap from her eyes when it dribbled from her head. A sudden draft of air startled her.

"Chara, what the hell are you doing? Didn't you hear . . . ?" Quentin roared, then his voice faded until there was only the rushing sound of the water.

Flustered, Chara tried to cover herself and wipe the soap from her face at the same time. Some of the soap reached her eyes. The sharp sting made her yelp and turn her face into the water. Through the noise of the spray she heard Quentin's laugh, firing her temper. Reaching up, she grabbed at the shower head, turning it in the direction of Quentin's voice. When she heard his shout, she knew a deep satisfaction which didn't last long. She felt his iron fingers gripping her waist.

"Want to play, do you? All right, I guess I can use a shower. I was going to take one after lunch anyway. This seems to be a specialty of yours, angel, luring me into a bath or shower, not that I'm complaining, you understand." Quentin's hard laughter threaded his voice.

Struggling to get at her towel and out of there, Chara

79

came right up against the wall of Quentin's bare chest. Forgetting about trying to wash out her eyes, Chara kept them closed and tried to slide around him. His hands slid to her hips, dragging her closer, making her realize that he had divested himself of his jeans in record time.

"Why didn't I remember how much I enjoyed this, little bride? What a lovely idea! I think we should do this all the time. Umm, you feel slippery. Are you going to loofah my back?" Quentin whispered, a slight hoarseness in his voice.

Chara tried to lean away from him but only succeeded in pressing her lower body more tightly to him. "Quent, let me go. I'm through now."

"I'm not, darling," he mumbled at her neck.

When Chara pulled away to protest, his mouth fastened tight, in the familiar intimate way.

"Chara, you have a lovely body." Quent breathed, his hands restless and seeking on her body.

She moaned in despair as she felt her own body take fire. How she wished she could resist him! July Fourth was going on in her stomach and head. Standing on tiptoe, she took hold of his hair. She felt him stiffen as though he expected her to yank it, but her fingers twined the hair tight, bringing him closer. Chara heard him groan even as he wrapped her tighter to his torso. Her hands stroked him, pressed him, dug at him. Never had she thought a human body could be so exciting as Quentin's. She loved the throbbing that was building in herself.

"I want you, Chara. I never have enough of you," Quent said, his voice muffled against her neck.

His words froze her. She wrenched herself free of his hold. "Your wants are not of prime importance to me, Quent," Chara said, her voice shaking, her mind screaming that she wanted him to love her, not just want her like the glorified mistress she was. "Since we have a busy day, I suggest you take a shower . . . alone. And make it a cold

80

one." She edged past, trying not to look at the muscle jumping in his cheek.

She dressed in record time, then went out onto the sunny patio to dry her hair. She was brushing it over her head when a cold-eyed Quentin came outside with a plate of sandwiches and a jug of lemonade.

They ate in silence, not looking at one another; then Quentin went inside, leaving Chara to clean up. When she finished, she rubbed nervous hands down the sides of her purple cotton jeans. She twitched at the demure lace collar of the apricot and lavender cotton blouse she was wearing. Lifting her chin at a defiant angle, she marched from the kitchen down the short hallway and out to the garage.

Quentin was watching her through narrow eyes, his arms resting on the steering wheel of the jeep. Gulliver was sitting in the back of the jeep, his leash tied to the seat. His tail thumped a welcome.

"Well, are you getting in, Chara? I'd like to get moving."

Grabbing the roll bar, she scrambled into the jeep, looking at the dog over her shoulder. "Will he be all right, Quent? Won't it bother him to ride in an open jeep?"

For a moment Quentin was still and stared at Chara. Then he jammed the gearshift in reverse, making the jeep almost hop out of the garage. "What would I have to do to get some of that tenderness in your voice when you talk to me, Chara? Jump off a high building?" Quentin's cynical laugh peeled her temper raw.

"Why don't you just stop being so . . . so nasty all the time." Chara gulped, angered that her voice broke a little. How she hated him! He always made her feel so weak and upset. She knew he was staring at her, but she didn't turn her head but gnashed her teeth as she tried to be as controlled as he was.

"All right, little bride, we'll call a truce."

"We're always doing that, Quent. Truces don't work with us."

He gave a harsh laugh. "Maybe you're right, but we had better try anyway. We have to get Gulliver to the vet."

Chara nodded, then concentrated on looking at the passing scenery. She wished now that she had thought to bring a hat or scarf. Her hair blew all over her face and she spent her time holding it back with both hands.

Cayuga Lake sparkled in the sunlight, the crystal-clear depths mirroring the azure sky. The green of pine and oak bent in a graceful ballet to the summer breeze. The twisting highway running along the lake let them view the billowing sails of every size and color skipping over the rippling water. Chara sighed, knowing that she would miss this place when she had to return to L.A.

By the time they reached the veterinarian, located on the outskirts of town, Chara was thoroughly windblown.

To their surprise Gulliver seemed happy enough to get out of the jeep and accompany them. When Quentin opened the door, the cacophony of barking, whining, and meowing stiffened Gulliver's legs into the ground. With Chara pushing and Quentin tugging, they were finally able to get the recalcitrant dog into the office. Chara slid by a Doberman pinscher, snarling but held in check by his master. One woman cradled her Pekingese called Snookums. A young girl and her mother protected a full-grown tabby that hissed at Gulliver from the protection of a blanket.

"Can you hold him, Chara, while I give the receptionist the necessary information?"

"Yes." Chara gasped, her arms looped tight around a loudly panting Gulliver, who every few minutes rolled his eyes up at her as though begging to leave.

It was noisy but seemed in control to Chara, who was glad there were only three patients in front of them. She wasn't even worried when the door opened and a woman walked in with a flawlessly groomed white miniature poodle who seemed to have impeccable manners. Chara let her gaze rest for a moment on Quentin, who had his back to the rest of the room. All at once the poodle froze, standing in front of Gulliver, its dark eyes fixed on the cat.

"Oh, dear," the owner of the white poodle said. "Bebe does not like cats of any—" The rest of the highly perfumed lady's words were drowned in an ocean of roars and growls, hisses and screeches, as the poodle launched itself at the offending feline. The Doberman took instant exception and hurled forward against his choke chain. Panting, Gulliver sensed a threat to Chara and lifted himself in front of her with a roar.

Quentin wheeled around, seeing Chara almost astride an incensed Gulliver. "What the hell   " he shouted, trying to reach Chara just as the frightened poodle decided on retreat, right through Quentin's legs. As Chara watched open-mouthed, Quentin seemed to rise in the air, trying to steady himself, but the leash was his undoing. The sequin-covered leather wrapped itself around his left leg and jerked him to the floor almost at Gulliver's feet. Delighted at the return of his favorite man, the dog began to lick his face.

Quentin was shouting. The white poodle owner was screeching.

"Chara, for God's sake . . . pull him away."

"You monster, look what you have done to my Bebe. Philistine. Sadist. Come to Mummy, darling. Did that bad man hurt my sweetie?"

Chara fought hard to control the bubble of laughter as Quentin pulled himself to his feet and fended off the perfumed lady at the same time. Every time Quentin threw her a murderous look, she had to bite hard on her quivering lips. Gulliver sat almost at Quentin's feet, his big head swinging first to his man, whose usually soft voice was now biting off words as though they were bullets. Then the barrel-sized black head would turn with interest to listen to the wildly gesticulating woman.

"How dare you say that my Bebe is a brainless idiot, you . . . you crass farmer."

"Madame, that foolish dog started a riot in here."

Chara sat back in her chair, her knees pressed to the sides of well-behaved Gulliver, both hands pressed to her mouth, as she shook with laughter.

By the time it was their turn, an icy calm prevailed in the office. The vet, Dr. Foster, assured them that Gulliver was in the best of health despite his misadventure with the trap. To be on the safe side the vet then gave Gulliver a series of shots. He also said that he had never encountered the dog before that moment.

Quentin's answers were clipped and curt. He glared at Chara if she attempted to speak. Chara noticed the twinkle in Dr. Foster's eye as they were leaving. Her answering grin was irrepressible. The silence between them was explosive when they returned to the car. Chara was glad when Gulliver put his head between them, wanting to be petted.

"Such a nice boy. Didn't even move when you got your shots," Chara crooned.

"No doubt he was exhausted after all the exercise he had in the reception room," Quentin grated.

"Really? I thought you were the one who did all the exercising, Quent. Was that a modified arabesque you did?" Chara burbled.

"I think it's called a free fall," Quentin hissed, his hard-eyed glance swiveling to Chara before switching back to the road.

The laughter burst from Chara, startling Gulliver.

Quentin's hands clenched the wheel, but Chara saw his lips quiver before a shout of laughter escaped him. "Damn you, Chara, for sitting there laughing while that old harridan chewed me up. The next time we bring Gulliver to the vet's, I'll sit in the jeep with him until it's our turn."

Chara caught her breath. The next time, Quentin had said. Would there be a next time? Chara pulled at her lip with her teeth as she thought how much she would miss Gulliver and Quentin. Even as the thought surfaced, it surprised her. She would miss Quentin. She wanted to be with him.

"Chara? Chara, quit daydreaming. Would you like to stop and have an ice cream?"

Chara stiffened. "Don't patronize me, Quent. I'm not a baby you have to buy a treat for."

"Don't be so prickly. I'd like an ice cream. I'm sure Gulliver would like one. There's a Friendly's up here. We'll stop and get a couple of cones. They'll put Gulliver's in a dish, then we'll hold it for him."

Gulliver almost swallowed all his vanilla ice cream in one gulp. He was more than willing to start on theirs when he finished his.

It was Quentin's turn to laugh when the big dog dribbled and drooled on Chara's shirt. When she protested, he licked her face.

By the time they reached home they were on amicable terms, much to Chara's relief.

Hot and grimy, they decided to take a swim.

When Chara donned the deep blue micro-bikini that Quentin had purchased for her in New York, she realized it was even skimpier than the one she had taken from home. Not for the first time she decried her too rounded curves, wishing that she were thin and interesting-looking. She was sure that too much of her bosom showed, but then shrugged, realizing that Quentin was used to women who wore far less. They probably wore nothing when they were with him, Chara mused, wondering at the flash of anger as she thought this, then groaned as she admitted jealousy.

Turning away from the mirror, she flounced out of her

room and out to the garage, where Quentin was sitting in the jeep, a panting Gulliver in the back.

His hard eyes raked her up and down until Chara could feel herself redden.

"You don't have to stare like that. Everybody wears bikinis nowadays."

"So they do. Get in, Chara."

Chara sighed at the clipped tones, wondering what made him mad this time. He was so unpredictable.

The crystal-clear lake was gasping cold at first but so invigorating that Chara wanted to shout out loud. Quick strokes carried her out into deep water; a strong desire was within her to swim out as far as she could.

Something soft caressed her bare abdomen. Even as she stiffened, Quentin surfaced in front of her, part of his submerged body still under hers.

"Not so far out, mermaid. Come on, we'll swim parallel to the shore. How do you like swimming in fresh water after being an ocean-goer for so long, Chara?" Quentin asked, seeming to speak with no difficulty even as he swam.

Chara found that water entered her mouth if she said more than a few words, so she contented herself with nodding.

When Quentin laughed at her, she reached over and pushed his head beneath the water. Then, turning, knowing he would retaliate, Chara sped back the way they had come.

She made it almost to the jetty, but the hand around her ankle pulled her back. Sputtering and coughing, she turned to push against Quentin's chest, laughing and gasping for breath at the same time.

"Don't . . . don't, Quent, don't duck me . . ." Chara laughed, not expecting him to listen to her.

"Give me one reason why I shouldn't. No, better yet, I'll let you go for a forfeit." Quentin spoke, easily holding her in the water, though Chara knew it was over both their heads.

"What kind of forfeit?" Chara whispered, her eyes wary.

Quent laughed. "Don't look at me like you expect to be thrown to the sharks. There aren't any in Cayuga Lake."

"What forfeit, Quent?" Chara badgered, not put off by his banter.

"Well, one kiss from my mermaid might do it. Just a kiss, Chara, not an orgy on the beach," Quentin said steelly. "I am your husband, or have you forgotten?"

"Not as hard as I try," she hissed.

His hard laugh acknowledged the hit. "Chara? Are we going to tread water out here indefinitely? Not that I mind holding you, wife, even if you do have a shrewish tongue, but there is a limit to my restraint."

"Really? I would never have guessed it," Chara riposted, leaning back from him.

"The hell with it," Quentin grated, his fingers biting into her. "You're a damn tease, Chara."

When Quentin's mouth dropped to hers, she felt the familiar excitement at once. She gave herself up to the enjoyment of it. She felt rather than heard Quentin's groan of pleasure as her tongue explored his. She felt no fear as she felt the water overhead. Tiny little candles exploded in her veins as his hands slid over her water-slick body.

Only lack of oxygen made them surface, but still Quentin didn't release her. Her body moved in the water in rhythm with his.

A boat horn tooted. There were shouts and catcalls. Chara pulled back.

Quentin looked at her narrowed eyes. "You are a damn tease, Chara." Then he flung away from her in a diving turn that took him far out into the lake.

Chara swam toward the cypress ladder on the jetty. She welcomed the heat radiating from the asphalt as it soaked into her body when she spread a towel and stretched out, still fuming at Quentin's words.

She gave a yelp as a sodden Gulliver decided to shake off his excess water while standing next to her. Jumping to her feet, she glared at the panting dog. "You're as uncaring as he is, do you know that, Gulliver?" Chara sputtered, feeling teary and despising herself for the feeling.

Gulliver's ebony coat, shining with moisture, shook from head to tail as the dog wagged his agreement to everything she said.

Once on her feet Chara was too restless to settle back on the towel. Quentin's words kept drilling through her mind, making her angrier by the minute. She started to wander up the beach, picking up fossils with one hand and rubbing the towel into her hair with the other. The fossilized rocks, with their unmistakable markings that identified a shell or a small creature or part of a larger animal embedded therein, intrigued her. After a few minutes she had a substantial pile of fossils and another pile of mineralized, colored stones. She had a sudden wish to know more about the subject of geology. She knelt in front of her cache, admiring it.

Idly she looked up from her rock collecting and watched Gulliver nuzzle his way along the cliff base. Then, while she was still watching him, he decided to follow a scent up the cliff face. It was steep and tufted in quick grasses, poison ivy, and assorted stumpy bushes.

"Come back here, Gulliver," Chara called, still holding the towel to her head with one hand. "Come down from there this minute."

She didn't know Quentin was behind her until she felt his hand on the towel. She stiffened, rising to her feet and backing away from him.

"What is it, Chara?" Quentin sighed, an irritated look on his face.

"I'm not a tease. I don't like being called names like that. That is what is the matter." Chara clipped her words, not bothering to disguise her anger. "Your problem, Quent," she pushed on, "is that you are too used to one kind of woman, those Gomorrah graduates in Hollywood. Well, I'm not one of those and I resent your lumping me with the cheap whores you're used to . . ." Chara gulped a deep breath, turning away from him to look at the dog, who was still climbing in a traverse fashion up the cliff face.

"Damn you, Chara, you've got a cutting tongue," Quentin began.

"And I've had enough of your damning me in every sentence too, buster."

A reluctant smile broke Quentin's irritation. "A little tiger, aren't you? You've sure sharpened your claws on me. I can't ever remember taking so much verbal abuse from a woman."

"If you can't take it, don't dish it out," Chara threw at him.

"All right, all right, Chara. I was out of line. I shouldn't have said that to you. I'm sorry." Quentin reached over and took the towel from her head. "Here, let me do that." He turned his head to look up at the dog. "Come down from there, you fool, before you break your neck. Hurry up." Quentin turned back to her. "Come back to the jetty, Chara. It's warmer."

Once more on the wide dock, Quentin massaged Chara's head. At first she held herself aloof, but gradually the heat of the sun and the even pattern of the rubbing relaxed her. They sank together onto Chara's bath sheet. Her head, bobbing back and forth, kept Chara from looking at him. She felt sleepy but had no idea she had dozed off until the moment she awoke and became aware that she was chilled. She lifted a hand to wipe her sleep-filled eyes and felt something heavy pinning her arm. She lifted her head and saw Quentin's arm across her middle. She turned her head and almost touched his face with hers. He was asleep, his lips slightly parted, lying on his side. Chara realized that her head had been pillowed on his other arm. She was sure his arm must ache. Even as she looked at him, he opened his eyes, the sleep-glazed look fading, a cynical smile touching his lips.

"You were lovely to sleep with as usual, bride." He stretched upward, reclining on one elbow.

Chara scrambled to her feet, whistling for the dog. "Don't you think it's time we went home? What time does your sister expect us?"

Quentin shrugged, uncoiling to his feet. "She wants us for drinks about six. We have time," he said, his eyes narrowing on her.

Chara had been glad to avoid Quentin while they were getting ready. He was in one of his black moods; his Arctic tones when he did speak were so forbidding that she escaped to the patio as soon as she was dressed.

She twirled on the flagstones, knowing that the pleated silk dress in soft mauve was very flattering to her blond, blue-eyed coloring. Catching sight of herself in the half-closed sliding glass door, she twirled again, watching herself with pleasure. She had to admit that Quentin's taste was good, and she was glad that he insisted she have the dress. The simple V-necked style clung to her rounded form and enhanced her long, slender legs. Matching ankle-strap sandals made her feet and lower legs look quite fragile. Her hand lifted and touched the heart-shaped sapphire pendant that Quentin had given her, as she looked over the lake.

"Devastating, wife. You look quite beautiful," Quentin husked as he caught her slowly turning body. His eyes were an opaque silver, but he didn't seem to be angry. Chara was relieved.

90

The ride to his sister's took mere minutes, since her home was located on the same road as Quentin's but at the foot of the hill. It sat on a point of land that pushed out into the lake and, like Quentin's, it was framed in natural cedar shingles. It had a rough-hewn elegance that appealed to Chara. Before the jeep had come to a full stop, a vibrant, slim brunette with a thick braid down her back and uneven bangs across her forehead bounced onto the running board. "Uncle Q, you old dog. You finally got hooked." The happy child woman hugged Quentin, then looked across him at Chara. "Hi! Are you really his wife? I'm his niece Amy. I'll bet we'll be good friends. I can tell you all manner of things about Uncle Q. Can I take the jeep after dinner. Please? A bunch of us—"

Quentin reached out over the door and lifted Amy to the ground, then pushed open his door. Before he could come around and help her, Chara pushed open her door and hopped to the ground, her face pinking a little at the unnerving stare Amy was giving her.

A frowning Quentin came around the front of the jeep toward her. "You should have waited for me, Chara. With those high heels you might have tripped and fallen." As he pulled her toward Amy, his hold tightened. "Amy, meet Chara. Chara, this vision in pink is my niece and you can bet anything the reason she wants the jeep is because her dress matches that fright of a canopy that she and her friends draped over the top."

Chara smiled at the bantering argument that ensued between Quentin and Amy. Her initial reticence with Quentin's niece was dissipating in the fallout of Amy's bubbling disposition. Still, Chara didn't feel ignored while the other two playfully wrangled, because not once did Quentin loosen his hold on Chara's waist.

At the sound of a delighted squeal behind them, Quentin winced. Chara had to laugh at his expression. He looked pained but game.

He turned to Chara, his lips twisted. "You are about to meet the world's surrogate mother, my sister Clem, short for Clementine, if you can believe the cruelty of my parents to saddle anyone with such a name," Quentin told a bemused Chara as a graying copy of Amy thumped Quentin on the shoulder, then hugged him.

"You horrid wretch, making fun of my name again. As if you didn't know I was named for father's great-aunt Clementine." A laughing Clem turned to Chara as she said this, grasping Chara's hand in both of hers. "Of course the idea was that I would inherit the old harridan's estate. I'm sure father will hold it against me forever that she left it all in trust to an outrageously expensive pet cemetery."

Chara gave a trill of laughter and Clem's eyes widened. Then she turned back to her brother, not releasing Chara's hand.

"Quentin Gifford Wainwright, you've brought home a beauty, but of course she's too young for you," Clem pronounced slyly.

Everyone laughed but Quentin.

"Chara is twenty-five. She'll be twenty-six soon." Quentin said, his voice taut.

Amy and Clem guffawed and said they didn't believe it for one minute. Amy insisted that he must have stolen Chara from the local high school and that's why he had brought her East, to hide out. Amy and her mother kept up the gleeful taunting, but Chara just stared at Quentin. His cheeks were mottled a deep red, his lips pressed into a tight line.

Amy's yelp was a welcome distraction for Quentin, Chara was sure. "Uncle Q, is that the dog you were calling Mom about? My God, he looks bigger than I remembered and a great deal more respectable. Lord, when I saw him last he was positively ratty-looking. Whatever did you do to him?"

Quentin's hard smile softened to a real grin. "I don't take the credit for that. Chara's been shampooing him in the lake. Also my food bills have skyrocketed. God, he eats everything and anything. What is really horrible is that Chara buys him liver and fries it for him. Ugh, the smell." Quentin grimaced.

Chara shook her head at him. "Liver is good for you, Quent. You'd like it if you tried it. I love it."

Chara couldn't help smiling when both mother and daughter in the Turner family shuddered right along with Quentin.

"Let him come out of the jeep, Uncle Q," pleaded Amy, making cooing sounds to the panting Gulliver, who was now wagging his tail so hard his whole body was quivering.

Quentin whistled to Gulliver, who jumped from the jeep almost into Amy's arms. The Labrador strutted around the two women, obviously feeling very self-important at the fuss being made over him.

"I think we have ourselves a star," Quentin whispered into Chara's ear.

"Definitely. I think you should sign him to a long contract," Chara pronounced, feeling inordinately pleased when Quentin gave a shout of laughter.

Chara listened, mouth agape, as Amy and Clem teased Quentin on every subject. Instead of reacting with anger, he took it in his stride and gave back as good as he got. Chara remembered her own childhood with wincing clarity—the haughty disdain of her mother whenever she or Ken attempted to joke with her, the totally blank, uncomprehending looks from her father whenever he was approached in the same vein. She could not remember either her father or her mother ever teasing her or Ken in the loving, light-hearted way that seemed a way of life in the Wainwright clan. Her initial tension gave way to amusement, then to relaxation. When Clem led her out to the

93

screened patio that overlooked the lake and pressed a vodka and tonic into her hand, Chara was already feeling very much at home.

Just as Chara was taking a sip of her drink, Quentin reached down and took it from her suddenly nerveless fingers.

"I'll make you a plain one, darling. I know you prefer that," Quentin whispered, his voice husky and intimate. Despite his lowered tones, Chara was sure that both Amy and Clem heard him. She wriggled with discomfort at Amy's open-eyed look. Chara pressed her teeth on her bottom lip, annoyed with Quentin. It was true that she preferred not to drink spirits most of the time and especially before eating because it made her sleepy and headachy, but there was no reason for Quentin to make an issue of it, Chara argued to herself, in front of his family. She stiffened in resentment at what she felt was cavalier treatment.

While he held her glass loosely in his hand, Chara snatched it back again, spilling some of the liquid on Quentin's tight-fitting cotton jeans. His narrow-eyed stare told her he was angry, but Chara was too irritated to care. "When I'm through with this one, I'll let you make me another, Quent," she said just before he spun on his heel away from her.

There might have been long, tense moments if it hadn't been for Gulliver and his determined efforts to get hold of the canapés.

The arrival soon after of Clem's husband, Jack Turner, and their son, Dennis, forestalled any words Chara and Quentin might have had. Dinner was a barbecue affair with steaks and salad. While the fire was getting ready, Amy decided they would have a family volleyball game. It necessitated Quentin and Chara borrowing clothes to play in, but since Amy rode roughshod over every objection, the game was soon on. Chara was sure she had never laughed so hard or fallen so much. After the game she was sweaty and red-faced. Quentin decided she needed cooling off and threw her off the dock into the lake. While he was still laughing at her sputtering ire, Dennis threw his uncle in and Amy pushed Dennis in, who pulled her in after himself. Chara laughed and laughed.

Showered and relaxed, they sat down to dinner. Chara thought that things were back to normal until she saw Quentin glaring at her when she had her second glass of wine.

Chara concentrated so hard on ignoring Quentin, she didn't hear how her birthday was introduced into the conversation at the dinner table.

"Oh, that's great," Amy enthused, clapping her hands. "Let's all take Chara out for dinner. We can go to Taughannock Farms. Oh, it'll be fun. Then we'll all go to the new dance barn on 5 and 20. Come on, Dad, say we will. Uncle Q, please . . ."

Amy would not be denied. The Turners were so taken with the idea that Chara was sure they didn't even notice Quentin's lack of response, but she noticed and was very hurt by it. At least he could have pretended to like going, Chara grated to herself. *Damn and blast his arrogant hide, just sitting there smoking that thin cigar like His Royal Jackass himself.* Chara seethed, wanting to pull the cigar from his mouth and stomp it flat. Instead she lifted her chin and nodded yes to Amy that she too thought it sounded like great fun, especially the part about the dance barn.

The silence in the car as they drove home was crackling with animosity. Quentin spoke as they passed through the doorway from the garage to the house. "Was that an infantile way of getting at me, agreeing with Amy about your birthday?"

"No, it was not, but I don't expect you to believe me," Chara said coldly. "I know only too well that you wish they had dropped the subject of my birthday. It was written all over your face."

"Was it, really?" Quentin quizzed. "You can read my mind, can you?"

"Yes, yes, I can," Chara lashed back, swallowing the pain. "I damn well can read that mind of yours. How you regret marrying me, how trapped you feel, how . . . how you hated my being a virgin because you felt yourself forced to marry me." Chara panted, the burning hurt boiling to the surface. "Did you think I couldn't tell that you thought I was some kind of emotional cripple because I had no sexual experience? That I was some kind of freak because I hadn't had a man in my bed? Or did you think I was a lesbian maybe? Is that it?" Chara sobbed.

"Chara, shut up. Damn you, don't say another word. You don't know what the hell you're—" Quentin ground out furiously.

"Don't you tell me to shut up," Chara shouted back, lifting her fists to pummel his chest. "I won't shut up and . . . and don't you come near me, do you hear? Don't come near me . . ." Chara gulped, then turned and ran down the hall to her room, slamming the door and turning the key in the lock. She sobbed until sleep took her.

During the following days, the house on the bluff was like an armed camp. Chara kept herself still and aloof from Quentin, doing nothing with him unless she had to and only speaking when necessary. Quentin's hard, silver eyes followed her whenever she was in the same room with him, but he too only spoke when it was necessary. Gulliver seemed to be the only happy member of the household. Chara knew with dread certainty that Quentin would be glad when she was out of his life forever.

Late in the afternoon of the day of her birthday, Chara had finished showering and was sitting with a towel around her head, buffing her nails. She had made up her mind that she would go down to the Turner house with or without Quentin.

When she looked up and saw him standing in the doorway of the bedroom, it was almost as though she had conjured him up.

"Happy birthday, Chara. I've brought you something," Quent said, his hand going to his inside jacket pocket as he walked across the room toward her. He stood in front of her for a moment, then dropped the package in her lap. He looked around the room for a moment, his eyes lighting on the rose pink sari that Chara had draped over a hanger on the clothes tree.

"I'm glad you're going to wear the dress I asked you to wear," Quentin husked, his one hand snaking around her neck as he bent above her. Chara didn't hear the words he muttered against her mouth because almost at once she was submerged in the electric sensations his touch always evoked. Before Chara could recover her equilibrium when he released her, he had turned and left the room.

With shaking hands she applied the rest of her makeup and then brushed her hair until it shone before twisting it into a coronet on top of her head.

Dressed in the rose silk sari that Quentin had bought for her in the India import store in New York, she fingered the pink jade necklace that he had just given her. She twisted her head to look at the matching dangling earrings. No wonder he had insisted that she keep this dress for her birthday. He had been planning to give her the jade, Chara mused, pleased in spite of herself.

The cocktail hour at the Turners relaxed Chara even more and this time Quentin didn't try to remove the drink from her hand. She laughed with Dennis and felt pleased at his obvious admiration.

On the fourteen-mile ride to the restaurant that faced the lake just below Taughannock Falls, a torrent of water that was higher than Niagara Falls, Amy told her, Chara found herself on the front seat between Jack, who drove, and Quentin. She was aware the entire drive of the pressure of Quentin's thigh against her and the light massaging of his fingers on her shoulder.

The dinner itself was delicious, but Chara could not have remembered what she ate. The entire dining room applauded with their table when a beautiful cake with one large sparkler candle was brought to it. Chara caught Quentin's sardonic smile and knew he had arranged it. She felt as though all the hidden feelings she had about Quentin had somehow fought free and were coming through her skin. Champagne sparkled into glasses as the cake was cut. Chara tried to listen attentively as Jack told her that the grapes for the champagne were grown on her own land, hers and Quentin's. She felt in tune with the universe as they rose to leave and vigorously seconded Amy's desire to visit The Dance Pit. Quentin said nothing, but she could feel his hand rubbing her waist.

Before they left the restaurant, Amy and Clem insisted she take a tour of the upstairs of the mansion. Clem assured her it was filled with splendid antiques. Somehow Chara became separated from the others, so she started down a staircase she found in a side hall. She was relieved when she heard Jack's and Quentin's voices. When she heard her name mentioned, she paused.

"I mean it, Quent. I almost passed out when Clem told me you were married and I sure never expected anyone like Chara. She's terrific. We all like her."

"I like her myself." Quentin laughed. "Come on, let's find the girls and that son of yours."

"All right. By the way, a man by the name of Judson called, said he was your production assistant. This was before you returned from sailing today. Clem no doubt forgot to tell you he called us when he couldn't get you."

"She forgot. I keep meaning to get an answering service for the lake house, but I never get around to it. I'll call

98

tonight when we arrive home. Thanks, Jack." The voices faded.

Chara grimaced. *So he likes you,* she mused. It's better than nothing. She shrugged, determined to enjoy her birthday, and joined the others.

When they dropped Clem and Jack back at the house, Jack stopped them for a moment. "Chara, I have to fly to New York early tomorrow, so I won't be seeing you again until Christmas. It was wonderful meeting the woman who tamed Q Wainwright. Have a nice evening."

Quentin was driving Jack's car. Dennis leaned forward from the back to give him directions.

The blast of sound as they entered the barnlike structure made Chara reel. She could barely hear Amy's voice over the din.

"Isn't it great, Chara? This was once a greenhouse. See the big tree in the middle of the floor."

Soon they were surrounded by Amy's and Dennis's friends. Chara danced with a gangling young man with hornrimmed glasses who informed her that he was a senior at Eisenhower College. She sighed with relief when Quentin rescued her from a rather round young man who was majoring in math at Cornell University.

"I couldn't let you dance with anyone else to this song. Sing to me, darling." Quentin breathed in her ear.

Chara hesitated, but then at Quentin's whispered "please" she softly voiced the words to the love song they had danced to in Vegas. She was unaware of how long they moved to the music, their arms locked around each other. She was happy to stay that way, delighting in the movement of their bodies.

Amy and Dennis decided to stay and ride home with friends when Quentin and Chara left.

In the car Quentin clamped her close to his side while he drove with one arm. Chara mumbled something about Quentin getting arrested for driving that way, then she gave up and snuggled her face into his shoulder. She felt his lips in her hair. Feeling reckless, she rubbed her hand on his thigh, wanting to stay close to him forever.

"Chara, either stop that or I'll be pulling over to the side of the road," he growled, his voice shaking. "I'm out of my depth with you, witch."

The ride was over too soon. She never wanted to tear her dreamy gaze from the reflections in the windshield. She wanted to stay wrapped in Quentin's arms. He was her world.

She felt dazed when he lifted her from the car and into his arms. She wrapped her arms around his neck, letting her lips rest against his ear. "I'm too heavy, Quent."

"No. You're just right, Chara, love," he answered, his voice hoarse.

Quentin allowed her legs to touch the floor when they reached the airy sitting room. He kissed her lingeringly before going to the sideboard and making them each a drink. Chara noticed that he put nothing in her bitter orange but added gin to his own. Feeling detached from earth, she let him lead her out onto the patio and pull her down beside him on the wide lounger that could easily hold three people. In silence they watched the flickering fires that lined the beach on the opposite side of the lake. When Quentin took the drink from her hand and turned her into his arms, she sensed a difference in him. His eyes were a sterling glitter as he eased her back on the lounger, making her gasp.

"You drive me mad, Chara, do you know that? My God, I don't know what to do about you," Quent said, his voice thick, his mouth feathering her cheek.

His words penetrated her skin, galloping through her bloodstream, choking her, making her come more alive than she had ever been. She felt as though she had shucked her skin, her insides, her mind, her spirit. She was reborn because she had given her love to a stranger.

He lifted his head, his breathing labored, and stared down at her. What she saw in his face started a trembling she couldn't control. A languorous weakness made her limbs leadlike.

"You were so beautiful tonight, little bride." Quentin's tones were sober, as though he were having a struggle of his own. His hand traced her from breast to hip, his fingers loosening the folds of the sari, his eyes staying on the rounded form exposed to his hungry gaze.

"Quent . . ." Chara choked, her hands reaching up to clutch at his descending head. Their mouths met with force, parting at once. His mouth was urgent, demanding, but the tongue that coaxed a response was devastating in its gentleness. Her arms, hands, legs were all new as sensation after sensation coursed her body, giving life. The warm, languid night air became charged. The stars dipped and swayed above them like an exquisite canopy. It had never been as wonderful as this.

Quentin pulled back. "Chara, darling, I'll take you to bed."

Chara felt a sudden anger that he would try to rupture their entwined delight. Unaware that her digging fingers could hurt him, she pulled him to her. "I love you, Quent," she whispered, awed at the profound truth of her words.

Groaning, he surrendered to her hands, her sensual touch turning him to flame as she gave herself to him.

CHAPTER FOUR

Bemused, Chara had let Quentin carry her to bed after their lovemaking. He had removed what little clothing they still had on and had gotten in bed beside her, enfolding her in his arms. Neither had spoken. Chara was too hazy with tiredness and the languid aftermath of making love. She fell asleep at once, content that Quentin was with her.

A coldness in the bed woke her during the night. She was alone. Her sleep-dazed eyes saw the blinking call light on the phone, forgetting that it flashed if someone was on the extension. She picked it up without thinking, and heard Quentin's voice. She was about to hang up when the caller said her name, then laughed. Almost against her will she listened.

"I'm telling you, Q, she's hard to handle. Ever since you married her daughter, Chara. What do you do now? Get rid of the daughter and marry the mother? God . . ."

"That's enough, Jud. Mind your own business. I'll handle Link and take care of my own wife as well," Quent snarled. "Now about the . . ."

Chara carefully replaced the receiver, her being turned

to ice. Quentin was carrying on with her mother while married to her! It was obscene. Her stomach churned and she thought she would be sick. She wanted to tear at Quentin with her nails. She had told him she loved him, had given herself in love, and he had every intention of carrying on with her *mother*. She had to get away. Jack. He was going to New York. She would go with him. She would go to England . . . and to Wendy. She threw some clothes into a suitcase. In the bottom of her jewel case she found her passport and rubbed it between fingers gone stiff. At first she was going to leave the dresses that Quentin bought her, then she thought better of it. She would need clothes in London until she could find a job. Even though she didn't anticipate going out in the evening, she added two of the after-six ensembles to the growing pile. She decided to take the one case with wheels and a vanity case. Finished, she looked around the room. She gave a gulping sob when she looked at the mussed bed where she and Quentin had slept.

Burning with humiliation, she covered her face with her hands and sank down on the vanity stool. Then she stiffened. What if Quentin came back to the room and saw her cases? She put them into the closet, then lay down on the bed, her body stiff. She would never see him again. Let him get the divorce. She wouldn't hold him. Restless, she looked at the clock. Five o'clock. Almost three hours had passed since she wakened. She lifted the phone cautiously, relieved to hear the dial tone. Where was Quentin? She got up and slipped down the hall, stopping in front of the study when she saw a light. The door was ajar, so she pushed it open farther. Quentin was sprawled across his desk, sleeping, a pencil still in his hand, papers strewn everywhere.

At six, fully dressed, she called Jack. She surprised herself by the cool explanation that she was meeting friends in New York. Then she hung up. England! She would have to see if she could get a flight. An adenoidal female said they had a cancellation. It would be held for her if she would just give her Visa number over the phone. Chara did.

The trip to Syracuse with Jack was an agony, but he seemed to accept her quietness as missing her husband.

He was very solicitous as he parted from her at the airport after she told him friends were meeting her. Chara hurried instead to another terminal to catch her flight to London.

Chara remembered little of the flight to Heathrow except that it was interminable. She had a terrible time getting a cab. When she finally reached Wendy's apartment, she was almost too wrung out to press the bell. It would be her luck if Wendy were away, Chara thought tiredly. When her friend opened the door, then enveloped her in a joyous hug, Chara could hardly control her tears.

Sharp-eyed, Wendy didn't ask for explanations, just bustled her friend into a bedroom, then almost forcibly put her into a hot bath while she insisted that she would unpack.

"Darling, it will be marvelous. Just the two of us again," Wendy enthused, tucking Chara into bed. "Phyllis is coming up to town this week, you remember my cousin Phyllis? Well, she is getting a divorce, takes forever here. Oh, Chara, did I say something wrong?" Wendy said contritely, taking the sobbing Chara in her arms. Without too much probing she was able to get the skeleton of the story from Chara. She knew that there was much Chara wasn't telling her. Like a good friend she refrained from asking.

For a few weeks Chara was content to let Wendy and Phyllis dictate her life, reacting like a sleepwalker to all suggestions. When she was there a month, she contacted her cousin Kermit and aunt Agnes and promised that she would come to dinner one evening.

"Really, Chara, if you don't eat something you'll be a

105

shadow. You've lost so much weight. Perhaps you're pushing yourself too much trying to get a job," Phyllis said, munching a sandwich. "If I were you, I'd just let that husband of yours support—"

"But you are not Chara, Phyllis, dear. Now take a damper." Wendy laughed, but her stare stayed fixed on her cousin for a few moments before she turned to Chara. "Don't listen to her, love. Her brother Tom, you know, the skinny one at our party last week, well, he said that you would make a great model. He should know. He works in advertising. You're so tall and slim, Chara."

Phyllis reluctantly nodded her head. "He did say that and he does know quite a few photographers. Anyway, I'd rather be me." Phyllis made a rude face and went into the kitchen for another sandwich.

Wendy tucked her feet under her on the couch and stared at Chara. "You know, you would make a good model. Shall I mention something to Tom?"

Chara shook her head and promptly forgot the conversation until the calls and letters started coming from Quentin. Panic-stricken, she refused the calls, wringing her hands as she tried to figure how he had traced her. She tore up the letters unopened. When Quentin told Wendy he was coming to England to talk to Chara, she became hysterical, blurting out to Wendy that he just wanted to come to settle on a divorce. She couldn't face him. When she insisted on finding her own place, Wendy called her cousin Tom.

Chara was turned down by several people she went to see about modeling jobs. By the time she went to see Grinnell Fallon, another acquaintance of Tom's, Chara was pretty discouraged. He was gruff with her but not unkind. He told her that he was one of the best fashion photographers in the business. Chara smiled but somehow believed him. She wanted to kiss his hand when he said that he thought he could use her.

To Chara's surprise she was a success. Grinnell was smug. "I knew those great cheekbones would do it. You're a mite too thin for real life, Chara, but not for the camera. You have that interesting ethereal look and you're tall. Nice, very nice."

In a short time, to her relief, she was able to get her own place, making Wendy and Phyllis promise they wouldn't tell Quentin where she was. She had no trouble extracting the same promise from her aunt and Kermit, whom she saw now and then. Their smug solicitude made her wince.

She began to go out evenings. First it was a duty that Grinnell assured her was good for her career. He took her to smart parties given by his clients, one of which was Exotica, Inc., the cosmetics firm that was one of his biggest accounts. Chara had become their latest lipstick girl, and the campaign had been a whirlwind schedule of sittings in the studio and outdoor sessions that had been chilling to Chara but wholly satisfying to a gleeful Grinnell.

She faced the evening with trepidation, still not able to deal with situations with her former confidence. Quentin was the specter in her life. He seemed to permeate everything she did. How he would laugh if he could hear Grinnell describe Chara as phenomenally successful.

When Grinnell approached her after depositing her coat in the vestibule, he had two drinks in his hand and a gentleman on either side of him. He handed one of the drinks to Chara and gestured to the shorter, bald man on his left. "Chara, this is James Fitzroy, the advertising director for Exotica."

"Miss Styles, this is a real pleasure." James Fitzroy spoke with a slight burr to his voice. "I have studied many of your pictures and I have to agree with Grinnell. You don't have a bad side."

Chara laughed, knowing she was blushing. She watched

Mr. Fitzroy's eyebrows lift, his eyes gleaming with interest.

"And, Chara, this is Ford Talbot, Exotica's chief executive. Ford, this is Chara Styles, the Pink Velvet Girl."

Chara turned to look at the taller man. He was slim and fair-haired. His sophisticated veneer and expertly cut clothes proclaimed his wealthy status. She was mildly intrigued.

His light blue eyes ran over her body assessingly from head to toe and back again, a smile of appreciation lighting his face. "I have also seen your pictures. They don't do you justice."

Chara kept the professional smile pinned to her lips even though she still had that uncomfortable feeling that stares like that gave her. She wondered if she would ever be able to throw it off completely. "How do you do, Mr. Talbot?" Chara said, her voice a trifle husky with nervousness. "Are you really Exotica's chief executive?" She posed the question, hoping it would distract him enough so he would forget about her for a moment and give her a chance to relax.

"Yes." He smiled at her as though he accepted her ploy and understood it. "I should amend that to say that I am the chief in this country. The parent company is in New York—Wainwright, Inc.," he said, taking a sip of his drink. Then his eyes narrowed on her. "Say, are you all right? You've gone pale." His free hand slipped around Chara's tiny waist.

She shook her head, swallowing, and moving back from him. "I'm fine. Really, I am. Just a little hungry perhaps. I forgot dinner tonight, Mr. Talbot." Chara's head was spinning. She watched the solicitous looks on the faces of the three men, but it was as though she were deaf to the words coming out of their mouths. "I . . . I beg your pardon, I didn't hear what you said."

"Never mind those other two, Chara. I'll take care of

you. First, I insist you call me Ford. Second, you come with me. I'm going to feed you. Grinnell, you take James over to the bar. Enjoy yourselves, gentlemen. I'll see you later. Food for you, young lady." Ford's voice brooked no argument. She followed him in docile fashion to the large table groaning with appetizers.

In moments Chara found herself with an array of canapés arranged by Ford on a large plate. She laughed when he insisted she try the deviled egg and also insisted on feeding it to her. She giggled when he wiped the corners of her mouth with a napkin to remove the remains of the egg.

When other people came over to be introduced to Chara, Ford made it obvious that he preferred to be alone with her. Soon there were no more interruptions.

She had a very good time the rest of the evening and didn't object when Ford said he was driving her home.

For the first time since leaving Quentin, she didn't face the night with dread. She had become almost resigned to the wide-awake nightmares that beset her as soon as the bed lamp was extinguished. That night after Ford left her, she faced her thoughts warily but with a new confidence bolstered by the eager way Ford had asked to see her again. She was getting over Quentin . . . not her hatred of him that she fed so carefully, but that stranglehold of love he had had on her.

Chara looked up at the darkened ceiling and smiled to herself, glad she would see Ford during the coming week. She closed her eyes and slept a deep, dreamless sleep.

Grinnell stared at her a long time when she breezed into his studio one morning and waved her hand in a happy hello. When she was attired in the pink satin figure-hugging gown that was her newest costume for Exotica, Grinnell came forward to adjust her elbow position and stopped in front of her.

"Whatever is doing it, Chara, keep it up." His grizzled beard seemed to quiver at her puzzled look. "You've come alive, baby. Maybe not all the way, but I see a small candle burning. The last pictures were sensational. If I'm not careful you'll make me a rich man."

Chara laughed, nodding at him, knowing he was her friend.

"Is it Talbot, Chara? Or shouldn't I ask? He's a few years older than you, you know." Grinnell squinted through the smoke of a cigarette, his voice gravelly.

"He's not as old . . . I mean he isn't much older than I am."

Grinnell's stare seemed to touch every plane of her fragile face. Chara could feel the redness that was staining her alabaster skin. "Don't worry, Chara, baby, I'm not going to pry into that precious secret of yours." Grinnell's mouth twisted into a semblance of a smile as he watched her open-mouthed reaction. "Oh, yes, I've known almost from the beginning that you're running from something or someone. The camera caught that lost look, that frightened, haunted gaze you have at times. It seems to be fading a little." Grinnell patted her hand. "Speaking as a friend, not as a cameraman, let me give you some advice, free for nothing, as you Yanks say. It's better to try and live than just survive. Put the bad behind you, Chara, girl. You know, at first I didn't think you were going to make it. Now I think you're on the upswing. I'm glad."

Chara nodded, swallowing hard. "Thank you for understanding, Grinnell. I'm very grateful for your friendship." Chara knew that she couldn't talk about Quentin to Grinnell.

He nodded as though he could read her mind, then turned away to rummage through the mess on his desk. "Ah, here it is. A message from your cousin Kermit. He said that he would be stopping by to give you a lift this evening." Grinnell grimaced at the note. "If I were you,

Chara, girl, I would run from that cousin of yours. Kinda scuzzy, I'd say."

Chara laughed, privately agreeing with Grinnell's blunt appraisal. The few times she had been in Kermit and Agnes's company she had felt uncomfortable, her skin prickling in distaste at their preoccupation with money.

The day flew by. Both Chara and Grinnell were tired but satisfied at the end of the session.

Getting ready for another evening spent in Kermit and Agnes's company is not really what you want, old girl, Chara chided herself as she studied her reflection in the full-length mirror, her body clad only in peach-colored bra and panties. Frowning at the slight protrusion of her hipbone, she reluctantly admitted to herself that she was too thin. Shrugging, she argued with herself that she was eating more since she met Ford, and, after all, she couldn't afford to get too heavy, not as heavy as she was before, when she was with Quentin. She photographed better on the thin side. Just a little more weight and she would look and feel just right.

When she heard Kermit's rather high-pitched tones, she hurried the last of her makeup. She stood there, twitching at her skirt, checking her sheer stockings for snags. Although she was quite unaware of her own beauty, Chara knew that she looked good in the restrained but glossily sophisticated makeup and the well-cut suit that enhanced her slenderness and height. The French twist that she wore defined her wide cheekbones and soft mouth with the too full lower lip. The white blouse with the frilly jabot drew attention to her long and graceful neck. With a sigh she left the dressing room, bracing herself to meet Kermit.

"Ah, there you are, Chara. Mother will be expecting us. Perhaps you could make your good-byes to . . . ah . . . Fallon." Kermit's patronizing tone made Chara squirm with a mixture of amusement and irritation. When she looked at Grinnell, she knew it was barely muffled

111

laughter making his beard quiver so hard. At once Chara had to put a hand to her own mouth to smother her mirth. She grabbed for her coat, urging Kermit to leave.

"Wait, Chara, let me help you don your coat," he said unctuously, making Grinnell bend over his desk, his sides heaving. "It's the end of November and quite nasty out there."

When Chara heard a muffled gasp from Grinnell, she gritted her teeth and didn't look back.

The drive to the house in an older section of the city didn't take long. The wealthy row houses were pallid to Chara's eye, but she knew that Kermit and Agnes were inordinately proud of their home.

"Chara, my dear, what a filthy night to be sure. Come in by the fire, dear." Agnes gushed.

Not for the first time the thought crossed Chara's mind that both Kermit and his mother considered her a mental incompetent.

The dinner was interminable to Chara. The only thing that seemed to interest mother and son was Chara's money.

Later, as they had tea by the fire, Agnes cleared her throat as she handed Chara her cup. "My dear Chara, have you thought any more about what we said to you about the . . . divorce. Now, dear, don't look that way. You know we would never intrude into your private life, but I do think you should sever connections with this Wainwright fellow before your fortune disappears."

"I've told you, Agnes, Quentin is much richer than I am and he is not one whit interested in my money. If you don't mind, I think I'd like to change the subject," Chara said, her voice weary.

"Well, my dear, we only have your best interests at heart, isn't that so, Kermit?" Agnes responded, an affronted look on her face.

"Er . . . uh, Mother's right, Chara. If you married me,

I would be more than happy to help you manage your money."

Kermit droned on in the same vein, but Chara wasn't listening. She was watching the ferretlike looks both mother and son were casting her way. All at once Chara felt ill. Ken had been right about one thing anyway, she thought—Kermit and his mother were most eager to get hold of her money. She knew that she would avoid any contact at all with them in the future.

Neither Kermit nor Agnes saw anything amiss when Chara pleaded a headache and asked to be taken home. She said good night at her door and slipped inside, shutting it behind her.

Undressing, she fumbled around for one of her two dressing gowns, then remembered she had dropped them both at the laundry that morning. Making a face, she donned her disreputable terry-cloth robe, feeling comfortable as she pushed her hands into the pockets as she headed for the shower. As she leaned over the tub to adjust the taps, she pulled a crumpled piece of paper from her pocket. Straightening, she idly opened it, then froze.

BRIDE, ENJOY. HOPE YOU LIKE MY TASTE. TOMOR-ROW YOUR TURN.

A sob rose in her throat as she pressed the crumpled note to her mouth. *Quent. Quent. What are you doing? Where are you? Do you laugh with other people about your stupid wife?* Chara agonized.

Tearing off the robe, the crumpled note back in the pocket, she stepped under the shower and turned it on blasting cold, trying to freeze all thought of Quentin from her mind.

The next day Grinnell was short with her. Chara was aware that she wasn't responding as well as she should.

113

"Chara, what the hell is the matter? You're back to square one. Relax, will you!"

She pressed shaking fingers to her closed eyelids, nodding. "I'll try, Grinnell. I'm sorry. I had a rather bad evening."

"That fry-faced cousin of yours is enough to put anyone in the doldrums. Why do you bother with him?" Grinnell mumbled, changing a position of one of his arc lamps.

"I decided last night I wasn't going to bother with either of them in the future. Are you ready for me?" Chara asked, taking a deep breath, with great effort pushing thoughts of Quentin deep into her mind.

They worked hard all through the afternoon until finally Grinnell called a halt. Chara felt like a dishrag.

"Sorry, love, but Exotica is screaming for those pictures. Speaking of the high-gloss folks, how are you getting along with His Nibs?" Grinnell quizzed, taking a gulp of scalding tea.

"Nosy little fellow, aren't you?" Chara smiled at the unabashed photographer. "I'm seeing him tonight, as a matter of fact. He's fun. I like him."

She was late arriving back at the apartment, but she was so tired she still allowed herself fifteen minutes to soak in the tub. She had washed her hair that morning, as she usually did, having discovered that her clean hair photographed vibrantly.

She threw open her closet and scanned the contents, deciding on a soft wool almost of a silky texture in a café au lait color that complemented her honey hair. Then she twisted her hair into a chignon. She enhanced the V-neck of the dress with a scarf of champagne silk with an abstract print of turquoise. She pushed an elongated turquoise ring that had come from New Mexico, Quent had told her, on her finger, and matching turquoise earrings through her pierced ears. She bit her lip as she gazed in the mirror at her reflection, hearing Quentin's voice as he told her about the Indian jewelry.

Relieved, when the doorbell rang, to leave her thoughts behind her, she greeted Ford with more warmth than usual. Delighted, he leaned down to brush his mouth across hers. Chara found the sensation pleasant.

"Actually you have a choice tonight, lovely lady. I have tickets to *Sparta*. You know, the modern tragedy directed by Quentin Wainwright that is burning up Broadway, so they say. It's expected to do as well here in London. Naturally Wainwright's purchased a block of tickets, good seats too. Or there's a new cabaret at a club downtown."

"As long as I have a choice, I'll take the cabaret. Livelier, I should think," Chara said, not wanting Ford to know that she just couldn't bear to see anything directed by Quentin.

"Now that surprises me," Ford said, an arrested look on his face. "I was sure you would have chosen the play. Lady, you never cease to amaze me."

Chara was glad they chose the cabaret. The singer was just average, but the comedian was bawdy and quite funny. Chara didn't have to think.

At her door Ford's good night kiss was insistent. Chara returned the pressure. He didn't seem to notice her lack of excitement.

"Chara, you're a darling. Exotica is having an early Christmas party. Will you go with me? It's for staff and board members too. I'm sure all of them know you by sight. It will make me so proud to introduce you to them."

Chara hesitated, then shrugged. It would be fun with Ford and she hadn't been to a party in a while. Besides, it was the Christmas season. Everyone would be attending parties now.

The night of the party it was snowing and there were Christmas lights in many of the shop windows. Chara left the studio early, promising to see Grinnell later at the party.

That night she added even more of her exotic bath oil to the water, loving the silkiness of her skin under the whisper of the black chiffon she chose to wear. Even though her body was incredibly slender, her breasts were still quite rounded and the black material, draped tight over the bodice, emphasized them. The figure-hugging skirt flowed soft over her ankles with a ruffled slit to the knee. It was simple, daring, and dramatic. She looked every inch a sophisticated model. She allowed her hair to fall to her shoulders, the soft curled-up blond strands caressing her exposed skin. She wore the sapphires that Quentin had given her for their wedding, swallowing the lump in her throat as she clasped the gold chain around her neck. Her fingers touched the sapphire heart nestled at the low neckline of her dress.

She smiled at Ford's wide-eyed admiration as he led her down to his car. She snuggled deeper into her velvet wrap at the coldness of the car.

She listened to Ford's easy banter during the short trip to the hotel where the party was being held with detached contentment.

They were directed to the party room by the stream of other laughing, well-dressed people preceding them down the hall. Chara was amused when some of them parted ranks to let them through, murmuring, "Good evening, Mr. Talbot," as they did so. Chara was also aware of the many admiring stares, both male and female, but she was getting used to that. Many of the Exotica personnel recognized her and some nodded by way of greeting.

At first the people around them spoke to them in a stilted way, but as more cocktails flowed, the talk was more informal. Chara sipped on her plain tonic and lime juice, answering the tentative questions put to her by some of the women about the modeling profession.

116

Ford stood proudly by her side, his hand lightly on her back. Even though he was conversing with a board member, Chara knew he was very aware of her. When his hand stiffened on her back and she heard his muffled "Well, I'll be damned," she turned to look up at him, then turned again to follow his stare.

"Hello, Chara, how are you?" As Quentin asked this, he deftly caught her glass of tonic and lime that was slipping from her nerveless fingers

CHAPTER FIVE

Ford seemed not to have noticed Quentin's greeting to Chara; his back-slapping hello to Quentin was boisterous and friendly. "I don't believe the almighty Wainwright himself is here. Chara, this is Quentin Wainwright. We went to Oxford together. Believe it or not, he still runs Wainwright, Inc., while being a movie director."

"Play director right now, Ford. How are you?" Quentin's sardonic tone was the same she remembered, his eyes the same Arctic gray. Chara noticed that there were deeper grooves near his mouth and a smattering of white hair near his temples. Had it been there before, she wondered, her mind hazy. Had his face always had such a bleak cast to it? When those silver eyes turned to her once more, she flinched. She could tell by the sudden tight smile that he had noticed the movement and knew why.

"That's a lovely dress, Chara. You look luscious, thinner—much thinner—but very sexy. Don't look surprised, Ford. I knew Chara in California when she was staying with her mother, Meta Lincoln Styles," Quentin explained, his words smooth, his eyes liquid silver as they roved over her.

"Your mother's Meta Lincoln Styles? I didn't know that, Chara." Ford spoke, his puzzled look going from Quentin to Chara.

"It just never came up." Chara shrugged, her hands clenching at her side. She looked around her as though seeking an escape route, when her eyes encountered Grinnell standing with three other people. He raised his glass to her, smiling, then frowned as though he could tell she was troubled. He moved to her side with relaxed speed.

"Dance, Chara?" Grinnell nodded to the other two frowning men, setting his drink down on a passing tray, his other hand clasping Chara's cold one. They glided around the floor silently. Chara clutched at Grinnell's shoulder as though it were a lifeline.

"Had a little problem, love?" Grinnell whispered in her ear.

"Yes . . . no. I don't want to talk about it, if you don't mind, Grinnell. Please, let's just dance," Chara pleaded with the smiling photographer.

"It's fine with me, Chara, but I don't think we'll be dancing very long. Quentin Wainwright is stalking us right now. Shall we make a run for the door?" Grinnell joked.

Chara was tempted to say yes and run for the door, but she knew that she would embarrass Grinnell, perhaps even damage his position with Exotica. Instead she gave him a sick smile and shook her head.

"My dance, I think," Quentin said behind her as he reached one hand to tap Grinnell on the shoulder. His hard-bitten words seemed to cut right into Chara.

When she turned into his arms, she kept her eyes lowered so that she was looking at his shirt front. She gasped when he pulled her tight to him, his head lowering, his cheek against her hair. Both her hands were imprisoned against his chest as they swayed to the slow ballad the band was playing.

120

"How are you, little bride? You don't look much like a paralegal lady anymore," Quent husked, holding her even closer.

"I'm . . . I'm not in paralegal work now. I'm modeling."

"I know, Chara. I've known right along what you were doing. Did you think you could hide from me?" he grated, his fingers digging into her back. "You're too damn thin. What the hell's wrong with you? I thought you had better sense than to go on one of those crazy diets."

I couldn't eat because of you, she wanted to scream at him, but she said nothing, just let her eyes rove the room.

"Look at me. Damn it, Chara, look at me, or I'll drag you out of here right now. Believe me, I'll do it," Quentin hissed, his head lifted back, staring down at her.

Chara was sure she could hear him grind his teeth, he was so furious. Steeling herself, she lifted her eyes by degrees, noting the faint grayness of his chin that even the closest shave didn't disguise, the strong nose, the nostrils dilating, finally the silver-quartz eyes that seemed to chill her blood. She swallowed twice before she spoke.

"There, I'm looking at you. What do you want? After all, I can hardly ignore the almighty Wainwright. My job as the Pink Velvet Girl could be in jeopardy, couldn't it?" Her voice was unsteady, but she didn't look away from him. A muscle jumped in his jaw as he turned her around the floor, not releasing her when the music stopped but continuing to look at her until another song began.

"Still the same nasty tongue you had before, little bride? I thought you might have outgrown that by now." He spoke, his tones acid.

Stung, Chara glared at him. "Why should I give up my nastiness when you haven't given up yours?" Chara snapped. "In fact you're even worse than you were. Let me go. Ford is looking this way. I'm sure he's wondering—"

"To hell with him. We're going to talk, Chara." Quent's

121

harsh tones were noticed by a few people dancing near them.

Uncomfortable under the searching stares of those around them, Chara wrenched herself free and proceeded to thread through the dancers as fast as she could. Blinded by her own misery, she failed to see Ford until she ran into him.

"Chara, Chara, what's wrong? What was going on . . ."

"Nothing . . . nothing was going on, Ford. I just have a frightful headache. I'll get something from the attendant in the ladies' room and be right back." Chara gulped, biting her lip, then turning from him almost at a run. In the ladies' room she let cold water run over her wrists, then soaked a towel in cold water, squeezed it out, and pressed it to her burning face. She kept repeating this until she felt calmer. She knew the attendant was watching her. She gave her a wan smile but didn't speak. She sat down on the bench in front of the large lighted mirror and attempted to repair her makeup, but her hand was shaking so much that she had to wait.

By the time she returned to the party it was much louder and the dancing quite energetic. Many of the people were flushed and some were unsteady. Chara hoped those would get a lift home and not drive.

"Chara . . ." Ford spoke at her elbow, startling her. "If you like we can leave now or—"

"Yes, yes, I'd like to leave now."

When Ford went for her wrap, Chara allowed herself to look around the ballroom-sized party area. At first she didn't see him, but when her eyes roved the dance floor twice she found him, a curvaceous brunette in bright red chiffon clinging to him, his head bent close to her pouting lips. Even as Chara watched, he looked up straight into her eyes, his face expressionless, then he leaned down and kissed the voluptuous woman in his arms.

Chara felt as though she had been stabbed with a hot knife. She hardly heard when Ford spoke to her on the way home, though she knew he wondered why she had run from the hotel without waiting for him to place her wrap around her.

She mumbled something at her door, then turned and went inside before Ford could say anything. She stood with her back pressed against it, her eyes closed, taking deep breaths. How long she stood there before there was a knock at the door, she wasn't sure. Sighing, she heaved herself away from the lock and turned to open it, sure it was Ford. When she saw Quentin standing there, she tried to close it, but he was too strong and propelled her back into the room without effort.

"What are you doing here? Get the hell out of here." Chara gasped, staggering, clutching at a high-backed chair to steady herself.

"Don't talk tough, Chara. I don't like it," Quentin grated, pushing one hand through his thick black hair as though he were gearing himself for battle.

"I only talk that way with you, Quentin. You bring out the worst in me. What I'd really like to do is punch your lights out," Chara sputtered at him, her chin thrust forward, wanting to strike him anywhere—face, arms, neck. Temper rolled her fingers into fists.

For a moment Chara was sure Quentin was going to hit her. All at once he gave a harsh laugh and shrugged. "Even if you have changed outwardly, you still have that same pugnacious temperament, don't you, little bride?" Quentin grinned, his saturnine looks making her heart flip like a trout on a line. "Aren't you going to ask me in?" he drawled, his eyes mocking the mulish look she knew was on her face.

"No. It's late. I don't entertain this late. Sorry."

"Then why were you so quick to open your door?" Quentin asked, his tone silky, his glance agate hard.

"Because I thought you were someone else—" Chara started to say, then gasped as his hand shot out and grasped her upper arm in a grip of iron.

"Who? Talbot? Does he come here often at night? Answer me, Chara." Quentin threw the words at her, his face savage, startling her. She shook her head, words choking in her throat.

"Why did you leave the party with him? You knew I wanted to talk with you," Quent shouted, not releasing her arm.

"I came to the party with him, so I left with him. It's none of your business, anyway. Now would you please leave?" Chara swallowed, her voice hoarse. She wrenched her arm from Quentin's grip and turned away.

"I'm not leaving, Chara." Quentin's voice was calm now.

"What do you mean you're not leaving?" Chara whirled to face him, her voice rising. "You can't stay here. My landlady won't allow that. She lives downstairs."

"Then you'll move to my flat." Quentin interrupted, a satisfied gleam in his eye. "Get your things together. Just take what you need tonight. I'll have someone come for the rest tomorrow."

"I can't . . . you can't . . ." Chara yelped, her eyes darting to every corner of the room as though she would find help somewhere. "I'm not going," Chara blurted out. "I won't fight you, you know. You can have the divorce. I don't want anything." Chara quavered, angry that she couldn't keep her voice steady.

"Shut up, Chara," Quentin grated, facing her, his features contorted. "I should beat the hell out of you for that, and the only thing that keeps me from doing it is that I don't hit women, but damn it, Chara, you make any more remarks like that and I'll change the rule of a lifetime. Now get this, you either come with me this minute or I'm staying. Believe it." Quentin threw himself down on the settee angled in front of the simulated fireplace.

Chara pressed one hand over her mouth, not knowing if she was going to scream with frustration or laugh at the ludicrous picture Quentin made on the delicate needle-point Victorian loveseat he was occupying. The loveseat was the pride and joy of Mrs. Charles, and Chara knew that the persnickety widow would have one of her spasms if she saw a man the size of Quentin on her precious furniture. Sighing, she lifted the hand from her mouth to her forehead, staring at her hard-eyed husband. "I will not sleep with you, Quent."

Such a look of violence crossed his face that she stepped back, but his tones were flat. "Get going, Chara. No more stalling. You and your landlady don't want me here, so get your things together. You're moving to my flat, little bride."

"Don't you call me that. Don't you dare call me that," Chara shouted, her voice verging on hysteria.

"Quiet down, Chara, and get packed before we have that old witch up here," Quentin said, as if the whole situation had begun to bore him. His eyes pierced her. "And don't worry about the sleeping arrangements . . . of any kind. You might not be sleeping with me, but you won't be sleeping with Talbot either. I'll see to that."

"You . . . you bastard," Chara hissed, wanting to tear his eyes out of his head, then throw him down the stairs. "How dare you speak to me in that fashion. I wish I were a man. I'd punch you senseless."

"Watch your language, you bad-tempered little bitch. And keep your voice down. It's bad enough dealing with you. I don't want to have to wrestle the old harridan downstairs."

"She isn't an old harridan," Chara spat at him, knowing that he had defeated her, that she would have to go with him or he would make it as awkward as he could with

Mrs. Charles. She ground her teeth at his knowing smile before she turned on her heel and flounced to the bedroom.

For a moment she toyed with the idea of climbing down the fire ladder and escaping, but as much as the idea appealed to her, she had no illusions about Quentin coming after her and dragging her to his place like a Neanderthal man dragging his kill.

She had the telephone in her hand, wanting to call Ford, but then she remembered the violence in Quentin's face when he mentioned Ford. She realized he would enjoy fighting with the other man.

When she returned to the small sitting room, Quentin was just rising from her small desk, a piece of paper in his hand.

"Where is your own stationery? With your name on it? I had to use this plain stuff because I couldn't find it," Quentin informed her, folding the paper and putting it into an envelope and sealing it. "I wrote a note for your landlady, telling her you would be gone until further notice."

Anger bubbled so strong in Chara that she had to take several deep breaths before she could speak. "How dare you! You're so bossy . . . dictatorial." She gasped. "As for the stationery, I don't use it because I've taken my maiden name back and the letterhead on the paper says Chara Wainwright." Chara took malicious satisfaction in telling Quentin this, pleased when she saw the red run under his skin.

"You *are* Chara Wainwright. Don't forget that. Even if you use your maiden name for modeling, you are still Chara Wainwright as long as we are married."

"Then let's get unmarried," Chara shot at him, waiting for the explosion she was sure would come.

"Let's go, Chara," Quentin said quietly, taking the overnight case from her nerveless fingers, then standing in

126

the open doorway waiting for her to pass through so that he could lock the door.

Fuming, Chara sped past him. *Damn him, damn him, damn him. I'll never understand him, never,* she steamed as she headed down the stairs and slammed out the door to the curb, not waiting for Quentin.

She let her eyes rove over the pale green leather interior of the Ferrari, trying to collect her thoughts.

"Amy wanted to be remembered to you when I saw you." Quentin's voice was low, his hands expert on the wheel as they traveled through the London night, crisp, cold, and clear.

"Oh, how is she? And Clem and Jack and Dennis? I wanted to write, but . . ." Chara faltered, her temper forgotten as she thought of Quentin's family.

"But you didn't want them to know where you were because you thought they would tell me, right?" Quentin's tones abraded her nerves, but she didn't respond. A far more important matter came to mind. She turned sideways on the seat to face Quentin. "How is Gulliver? Have you still kept him? Tell me about him."

Quentin turned to look at her anxious face, a real grin lighting his face. "You'd be proud of him, Chara. He's bigger and his coat is like velvet. He stays with Clem when I'm gone, but I try to get up there weekends when I'm in New York. He brought home a kitten." Quentin's laughter filled the car as he described the bedraggled thing Gulliver had brought home in his mouth. Chara rested her head against the cushioned leather, laughing as Quentin told her how devoted the huge dog was to the tiny ball of fur, letting it crawl over him and sleep on his back.

"He misses you, Chara. I can't explain why you're not there, so he keeps giving me those long looks that make me feel so guilty."

"Oh, I know the look you mean. Those big brown eyes looking like melting chocolate. Oh, dear, I miss him too.

I . . . I miss the lake. I thought how pretty it must have been in the fall."

"Spectacular, Chara, all reds and golds against the blue sky and water. Next fall we'll make sure we spend time there." He spoke, his voice firm, one hand reaching over to clasp her thigh in a light hold.

Chara swallowed, wanting to push his hand away, but reluctant to remove that exciting warmth from her body. She felt a shiver of feeling radiating from his fingers, filling her body and mind, soothing yet stimulating at the same time. She mumbled answers to Quentin's questions, hoping her responses were correct, somehow not able to free herself from her lassitude.

Blindly she allowed him to help her from the car in the underground garage, watching him while he brought both her cases into the elevator. She barely registered that the elevator opened into a private foyer where a very homespun woman, a starched apron making her look plumper, her gray hair in a tight topknot, bobbed a greeting.

"Good evening, Mrs. Jenkins, this is my wife, Chara. Chara, this is Mrs. Jenkins, our housekeeper. She and her husband take care of things for us. Mrs. Jenkins, could you have Jenkins get the rest of Mrs. Wainwright's things? They're in the boot. Come along, darling, I'll show you our room."

Red-faced, Chara gave Mrs. Jenkins a tight smile, her temper heating up again. She followed Quentin into another center hall that seemed to bisect the apartment. She almost bumped into Quentin when he stopped. Without setting down the valises he gestured with his chin.

"Living room and dining room to the right. Kitchen at the end of the hall with a smaller unit behind it for the Jenkinses. Library, or my hideaway, is on the left. The bedrooms are up that stairway over the library. The master suite is at the front with a large sitting room in between. Beyond are two smaller rooms. The living room

128

has a cathedral ceiling. I think you'll like the place, but if you don't, change it," Quentin drawled, his smile more pronounced as he looked back at her mutinous face. He was halfway up the stairs, carrying the two valises as though they were empty, before she spoke.

"Quent, how did you find me?" she asked, her voice low, but stopping him.

He looked down at her, his face cruel. "Your Visa card, for one thing, but there were other ways. Don't try to get away from me, Chara. You can't." He stared at her, then turned and went up to the room.

Chara gripped her night case as though it were Quentin's throat. She followed him into the mammoth bedroom, and was taken at once by the king-size bed covered with champagne silk, with walls and swag-back curtains the same champagne shade. Blue and turquoise throw pillows were scattered near the headboard as the only contrast. Chara found the serene effect appealing. "This is your room," she accused, closing the door behind her in case their voices might carry to Mrs. Jenkins. "I told you we are not sleeping together. I mean that, Quent. I'll take one of the other rooms."

"Don't spin your wheels, Chara. You can have this room. I'll sleep in the sitting room that adjoins this. The couch opens into a large bed," Quentin said, his look remote.

"Then why did you intimate to Mrs. Jenkins that we would be sharing a room? You have her thinking that we're . . . that it's a real marriage," she hissed, trying to keep her wobbling voice from rising.

"It *is* a real marriage, Chara. Until we get a divorce, it's a real marriage." He bit down hard on the words.

"But we don't . . . are not going to sleep together." Chara gulped, furious at his mocking smile.

"You do carry on about that, don't you, Chara? Even if we don't sleep together now, we did. It's a real marriage.

Don't forget, I have no intention of being grist for the gossip columns, so even in front of the live-in help I want it to appear that we have a normal relationship," Quentin grated, restraining his violence as he tossed her suitcases on the fine bedspread.

Protesting, Chara moved forward to move the suitcases to the floor, but Quentin forestalled her, his hands clasping her upper arms.

"Leave it, Chara. Do you understand what I'm saying to you? I want—"

Wrenching free of him, Chara interrupted angrily. "Yes, I understand you, Mr. Boss Man. I'm not really that stupid, Mr. Boss Man . . ."

"Chara, stop that," Quentin shouted. "Is it so wrong that I want to keep my private life really private?" He let his hands slide down her arms to take her hands in his.

"What makes you think Mrs. Jenkins or her husband would talk about you?" She quivered, trying not to respond when he lifted her hands to his mouth, his tongue touching the contours of her palms.

"Nothing." He shrugged. "I just don't want to take a chance. All right?

"Yes. All right." She nodded, pulling her hands from Quentin's. "But I think I should take the sitting room. You're too tall to sleep on an ordinary bed. I'll sleep on the couch, or I won't stay here at all. No, don't look like that, Quent. I mean it. I couldn't sleep knowing you were all doubled up on a regular bed. Please, let me have my way on this?" Chara's voice wobbled.

Before she could back away, Quentin had pulled her to him; the breath left her body as it came in contact with his muscular chest. His mouth hit hers like a ram. She tasted blood as his mouth explored hers with hunger. Her ineffectual struggles ceased as heat coursed through her own body. Her hands, as though with a will of their own, reached up to comb through his thick, curling hair. He gasped against her mouth, making her body melt against him. He pulled his lips from hers, then let them course down her cheek to her ear, nibbling at the sensitive lobe.

"Let me share your bed, little bride. What sweet memories we could make," Quentin said, his voice hoarse. Chara felt the heat draining from her body, leaving an awful coldness. Her hands came down from his head to thrust against his chest; the sudden motion made him stagger backward.

"Sweet memories! Something for you and your friends to laugh about. Maybe we could tape our lovemaking and then you could play it at the divorce party. How diverting." Chara gulped, her voice reedy as she tried to stifle the pain that was surging through her.

Chara bit her lip and stepped back at the rage silvering Quentin's eyes. A muscle worked in his jaw as he fought to control himself. She was so sure he would hit her, she brought up her hands up in a protective manner.

"Damn right you should try to defend yourself, you little bitch," Quentin ground at her, the icy rage making the bones in his face surge forward, his sun-browned skin almost saffron with fury. "Someday I'm going to tear out that waspish tongue by the roots." He breathed, stepping around her and plowing through the connecting door between the bedroom and the sitting room, the slamming of the door reverberating throughout like the last note of a death knell.

Chara stood, hugging herself, unable to stop her body from shaking. *Oh, God,* she moaned to herself, *how am I going to bear it . . . being in the same flat as Quent, loving him, wanting him, knowing that he will only want me for a short while before he goes on to someone else, probably a showgirl.* Chara pressed shaking hands to her eyes, trying to press out the thoughts of Quentin making love to someone else.

She shook her head, making moaning sounds to herself,

curling her body into a ball as she lay upon the bed. Her last thought was that she must fight him every step of the way, that Quentin must never discover how much she loved him.

CHAPTER SIX

When Chara awoke, stretching, she had no idea where she was for a moment. Then she remembered last night, falling asleep with her clothes on. Chara gave a muffled cry when she realized she was naked under the silken sheets. She could feel the heat in her body as she wondered if it was Quentin who had undressed her.

Shaking her head to push away her thoughts, she jumped out of bed, heading for the bathroom. Open-mouthed she looked around the cream-colored tiled room with its separate stalls for sauna and shower, a huge oval tub recessed in the floor with a raised tile deck surrounding it. "How like Quent to have a baby swimming pool for a tub," Chara muttered to herself as she gave the faucets a vicious turn, letting steaming water fill the area. Awed at the array of scents and oils for skin and tub, delighted to find that many were her favorites, she finally chose by saying "eeny, meenie, mynie, mo," giggling at her own childishness as she dropped down into the bubbling, fragrant depths.

She was just closing her eyes and leaning back against the bath pillow when a rustling and a splash snapped her eyes open. She tried to struggle to a sitting position when a hand slid across her abdomen and pushed her back.

"Stay still, darling. I'm going to wash you, then you can wash me. You're right, that bed in the sitting room isn't long enough for me. Do you think you'll mind changing with me? You looked so cozy in that big bed of mine," Quentin whispered close to her cheek as he rubbed a loofah down her arm. "Come lie with me and be my love. Isn't that what a poet said once?" Quentin growled into her ear. "Sleep with me, Chara."

Chara, horrified to have him there, latched onto what he first said to her. "I . . . I knew that the bed in the sitting room would be too small for you. I'll be glad to change with you," she gulped, hating having him there beside her, wanting to scream at him to leave her alone. Somehow the words wouldn't rise out of her clogged throat. His breath on her cheek and the rhythmic motions of the loofah were acting like a drug on her system. "Quent . . . Quent, listen to me for a moment. Last night when I *went* to bed at least, I didn't go to bed, I fell asleep with my clothes on. Did you undress me?"

"Of course, little bride. Would I let anyone else touch you like that, remove your clothes? No, you know that I wouldn't. I would resent even a woman's ministratio..s on your lovely form. You were delectable. You have no idea what it took to keep me from joining you there." Quentin's tones accompanied by that twist of a smile stiffened her spine; her temper started to simmer.

"You're unspeakable. Do you know that? Taking advantage of me when I was sleeping," Chara sputtered.

"Taking advantage, hell. If I had taken advantage, I would have woken you first, angel. I have no stomach for making love to sleeping women," Quentin barked, his hands like steel as he turned her face to his, kissing her hard and long.

Chara tried to resist him, but in seconds she was grip-

134

ping him to her, her mouth opening under his like a flower opening to the sun.

"See how it is with us, angel?" Quentin husked against her mouth, his one hand stroking her side. "We're fine together."

"No, no, we're not. And you shouldn't have undressed me last night and you shouldn't be here now," Chara stammered. "Get out while I finish my bath." Chara gulped, her voice rising, wanting to hit that cynical mouth of his.

"Finish. I won't stop you. I'll just take my own bath while I'm here. Pass that bar of soap, will you, Chara?" Quentin's words were clipped, but Chara could see the fury in those silver eyes—fury and something more.

Uncertain of his mood, Chara stared at him before she began to ease away and rise.

Quentin put his hands on her, sliding her body over to him, locking them together with gentle but firm hands. "You must have forgotten you were going to wash me. I washed you. Now it's your turn," he ordered, his eyes on her mouth.

Chara screamed at herself silently to tell him to go to hell. Instead, her traitorous hand took the loofah from him and began to run the soapy sponge down his one arm. She didn't look at him as she let the loofah run over his shoulders, but she could feel his hard gaze on her. She knew he was going to kiss her again, but she didn't move away or struggle as she watched his descending mouth. After all, she would need something to remember when he was out of her life, she argued with herself, reaching for him.

For a moment she was cool and aloof, but the silky water and his even silkier touch brought her senses to life. Perhaps she could have fought him if he had been rough with her, but he was gentle. She had the wild ridiculous sensation of being seduced again.

135

"You're lovely, little bride, you're beyond compare," Quentin whispered, his lips tracing a course from her cheek to her throat. His hands explored her body as though he were trying to reenforce a memory.

How expert he was at arousing her, Chara thought, as she sank deeper into a vortex of feeling. How many others had he made respond this way? What did he mean by beyond compare? The memory of her mother laughing as she described Quentin's power over women cooled her heated blood. She stiffened in his arms, but she realized that Quentin was not aware of that as he continued to caress her body, his hands moving with increasing urgency.

With one harsh thrust she pushed Quentin and rolled to her feet, grasping the slippery edge of the tub. She stepped out, skidding dangerously, before she turned to face him.

"What's the matter, Chara? What the hell are you doing?" Quentin hissed, his shining eyes narrowing on her supple form touched here and there with bath foam.

"Protecting myself from you, you . . . you bastard. Don't you touch me again." Chara gulped, her voice painful in her tight throat.

"You're my wife, Chara. That gives me the right to touch you, look at you, or anything else I want to do," Quent grated, letting his insolent gaze rove over her.

"No, I'm not your wife . . . or . . . I won't be soon. I'm not going to stay married to a man like you. I want a good husband."

"Like Talbot, you mean?" Quentin drawled, squeezing out the loofah in a crushing grip as he rose to his feet.

Chara could feel the heat in her body as she looked at the tall, muscled form entirely bronzed by the sun. She wondered whom Quentin had sunned in the nude with, then was surprised by the tearing jealousy that pained her body.

"Yes," she flung at him, wanting to wound him. "He's a better man than you could ever be."

At his threatening motion Chara turned and ran into the bedroom, grabbing at the clothes she had laid out, then sprinting into the sitting room, locking the door behind her. Out of breath and feeling nauseated, she sank down on the open Hide-a-bed and covered her face with shaking hands. She knew she had to get away. Another confrontation with Quentin like that and she knew she would fall apart

Since all her makeup was in the bedroom with Quentin she had to make do with just dressing and running her fingers through her hair. She made a moue into the mirror. She had fully intended to wash her hair while she had been in the bath, but Quentin had spiked that too. She felt vulnerable and exposed without the mask of makeup.

When she could no longer deny her hunger pangs, she left the sitting room and descended the short flight of stairs to the lower level. Remembering Quentin's description of the house, she made her way to the dining room, hesitating when she saw him bent over a newspaper, a steaming coffee cup in one hand. He spoke without lifting his head to look at her. "There are eggs, kippers, and tomatoes on the sideboard. Everything is freshly made, including the coffee. Help yourself."

"Thank you," Chara answered, her manner stiff, helping herself to fresh orange juice and a slice of rye toast that she spread liberally with black currant jam.

"You don't eat enough," Quent snapped, making her jump, her hand wobbling, spilling jam from the silver spoon onto the white table cover.

She looked up in mute anger, knowing from his smile he was fully aware of her ire and the cause. "Must you always bark at people? And for your information, I am not too thin and I eat enough. You're the one who spoils my appetite," Chara said waspishly, thinking how true it was, how she had missed him and wept over him when she first came to England. She swallowed at the flat, implacable look on his face. When she continued speaking, her voice was hoarse with the effort. "And . . . and I'm moving back to my own apartment. I don't want to stay here."

"Really? We'll see," Quentin said mildly, then looked at his watch and excused himself. She was still sitting at the table when she heard the outer door slam and knew he was gone. She was relieved and disappointed at the same time. Rubbing a weary hand across her eyes, she tried to make herself rise to dress and get ready to go down to the studio. Grinnell had warned her they were in for a long session today.

By the time she had dressed and had assured Mrs. Jenkins that any food she prepared for dinner would be just fine, that it wasn't necessary for her to check with Chara every day despite Mr. Wainwright's insistence to the contrary. They would let her know if they changed their plans.

When she arrived at Grinnell's studio, rushed and a little breathless, she noticed the high color on his usually pallid face, his myopic eyes snapping with excitement.

"Chara, girl, we made it. I got the call from Exotica this morning. They like the spread. Hang on to your hat. They want us—you and me—to come to New York. New York! Wow! I can't believe it. This could make a name for me, Chara. Say you'll come," Grinnell pleaded, his face creased with excitement.

Chara hesitated, wanting to say yes if only for Grinnell's sake. As she thought about it, it became more of an attraction. It was a way out for her. She could leave Quentin behind in London. "I, yes, I'm going to say yes, Grinnell. Have you ever been to New York? It's the most wonderful city." Chara smiled, infected by Grinnell's happiness.

He didn't answer her, just clasped her around the waist

and waltzed around the room, singing in an unmelodic tenor, "I love New York."

When Quentin called her during the session to tell her they were attending a dinner with some of his friends that evening, she said nothing about the New York trip, preferring to announce that in person.

On impulse she decided to shop for a dress on the short break Grinnell allowed her for lunch. Quickly downing the sliced tomato and cucumber sandwich and tall glass of buttermilk, she hurried around to a little shop run by a friend of Grinnell's. Mr. Giovanni had been an assistant stage manager when he had first come from Italy. After saving his money, he had opened a shop that catered to a small but rather select clientele. He and Chara had become friends almost at once after Grinnell's introduction.

"Chara, *cara mia.*" He greeted her as he usually did, telling her again that she should remove the "h" from her name so it would be Italian. "After all, is it not pronounced like the Italian *cara*? Ah, but that is not why you graced my small shop, is it? Come, I have something to show you. It is made from the wild silk that comes from India. It floats in the air and it is the color of your hair," Mr. Giovanni enthused, his hands clasped in ecstasy.

Chara held back, frowning. "I don't think that sounds like the color for me, Mr. G." When she saw his mobile face dissolve into sadness, she relented and followed him back to his workroom. With a very European flourish, he gave her the dress and urged her into a changing room.

Very skeptical, Chara slipped the filmy material in pale gold down her body, reveling in its richness. It clung to her body like a second skin, with a sensuous flaring just below the hip line. It delineated and enhanced her every soft curve, baring her arms and plunging in a provocative V in front. It was starkly daring and the color made her skin bloom like a peach while it emphasized the texture

and sheen of her hair. Open-mouthed, she stared at her image, knowing that few gowns had suited her better but wondering if it was too daring to wear. What would Quent say, she wondered, then was angered at her feeling. What did it matter what he thought? She argued with her lip-biting image. She twirled in front of the mirror and went to show Mr. G, who rolled his eyes and kissed his fingers in her direction. Laughing, Chara said that she would take it, then hurried to another friend of Mr. G's for the soft, strappy Italian sandals that she was assured would allow her to float like an angel on any dance floor.

When she arrived home, she was met by a tight-lipped Mrs. Jenkins, who said that she was most upset that Mr. Quentin had changed his dinner plans without consulting her and would Mrs. Wainwright speak to him about it?

After promising that she would, Chara escaped to her bedroom. With a sigh of contentment she immersed herself in a bubble bath and let the fragrant water soothe her. She knew she wouldn't totally relax in Quentin's company, but she was sure she would be able to cope with this evening armed with the knowledge that she would be leaving England and Quentin in a week's time.

She could hear him rustling and rummaging in the bedroom, but the door was locked to the bathroom, so she felt safe. He would use the other bathroom down the hall.

She gave a sigh of relief when she saw he wasn't around while she was dressing. Pawing gently through her jewel case, she found the set of topazes Quentin had bought in New York just after their marriage. Quentin had insisted that she must have jewelry and had overridden all her objections, dragging her to a jeweler friend of his on Forty-seventh Street in New York. Chara remembered how they had laughed when Quentin had draped a heavy ornate antique necklace of diamonds around her neck and called her Diamond Lil. Then they had had most of the jewelry sent by registered messenger, but Quentin had insisted that she wear the topazes because he was going to take her on an ocean cruise. He then proceeded to take her on the Staten Island ferry. Chara had been enchanted by the ride, thrilled to see the Statue of Liberty so close at hand. Chara remembered how they had waved to passengers on a real cruise ship leaving the harbor, not feeling a bit envious because she was held tight to Quentin's side by his muscular arm.

Chara shook herself from the reverie, absently rubbing some of the cream perfume that she had put behind her knees onto the pulse points of her wrist and throat and behind her ears.

Taking a deep breath, she descended to the first level and entered the living room, where Quentin was at the lighted bar pouring a drink, his back to her. Before she could say anything, he had turned, his eyes burning silver over her body, a muscle moving in his cheek.

"You're beautiful, Chara—delicate, luscious, and graceful." His tones were sardonic, but Chara could see the flicker of movement deep in his eyes that told her he was not unaffected by her appearance.

It gave her a heady sense of power, knowing she had such an effect on him. Surrendering to an impulse, she twirled in front of him, her heated body knowing that Quentin was watching her every move.

"Do you think it's cut too low in the back, Quent?" she asked, looking over her shoulder at him, suddenly breathless at the expression on his face.

"Yes. Back and front, but you look lovely, as I'm sure you know." He grinned at her all at once, his eyes dropping to scrutinize her body, then going back to her face. "I wonder if you know that that dress shows off that rounded derrière of yours almost as well as those cut-off jeans you wore when we went sailing," Quent drawled, coming up behind her and putting his lips to her bare shoulder.

141

"Don't be silly." Chara gasped, not moving as Quentin let his lips roam to her neck, then down her back, wishing that her body wouldn't play traitor and try to melt against him. "How . . . how can you remember those scruffy old things?"

"Easily, my love. There are many nights when they are part of my dreams. Would you like a drink?" Quentin inquired coolly, moving to the bar.

She was miffed by his ability to turn his feelings on and off when she was left shaken and upset. Her voice was curt when she answered him. "Yes, I'll have a dry sherry." Confused, she took the drink from his hand and stared up into his face. "Aren't you afraid I'll fall over drunk after this? You don't usually offer me anything. You must explain your hangup to me sometime," Chara babbled to a quick halt, seeing the hard look in his eyes.

For long moments Quentin stood in front of her, watching her broodingly, noting when her hand shook as she lifted the glass to her mouth. "Come and sit down, Chara, I want to tell you a story. It won't take long, but I think you should know it." Quentin led her to the overstuffed settee in front of the fireplace, easing her back into the nest of cushions, then sitting beside her, close but not touching. He cleared his throat and took another swallow of the whiskey in his glass. "About eighteen years ago, when I first landed in Hollywood and was struggling to make it as an actor—I originally tried out as a stunt man, did you know that, Chara?" Quent inquired huskily, almost as though he were avoiding coming to the point. At Chara's negative shake of her head, he cleared his throat once more. "Yes. I thought it would be pretty exciting, but then I found I didn't like risking my neck enough to get good at it. That's when I turned to acting. While studying at the Actor's School, I met a girl who was also studying acting. Her name was Jean—Jean Middleton. She came from Iowa, a farm. We liked each other right away . . . no, we

142

fell in love right away. We moved into an apartment together and it was great. We began to get a few parts and meet other people in the business. We started partying with them. Jean started drinking more and more, sometimes taking pills to help her get over the hangovers. She started missing morning calls, rehearsals." Quent was speaking fast, like the words were bitter gall he had to spit from his mouth. "One night I went home and found her dead on the floor. Her body was already stiff and cold." Quent blinked once, then rose to his feet and leaned against the fireplace, looking down into the flickering fire.

Chara watched, her throat constricted, wanting to run to him and comfort him but not sure if he would rebuff her. How he had hated telling her about Jean! How much he must have loved her! If only he had just a little of that love for her, Chara thought, biting her lip. "Quent, I'm sorry. I didn't know."

"Of course, you didn't know. My family didn't know until it was over. Jean and I only lived together four months. Four months! Do you hear that, Chara? It took only four months of constant drinking to kill Jean—not years—months. Even after all these years, I still can't believe it happened like that. It was like being on a roller coaster to hell."

"You must have loved each other very much," Chara said through stiff lips.

Quentin shrugged. "We thought we were in love, but we were damn young too. I'm thirty-eight years old now, Chara. I waited that long to marry. I don't fool myself that some of the cynical attitude I've always had toward marriage wasn't, if not born in my time with Jean, at least nurtured there."

"So that's why you hate to see me drink. I wish you had told me this before, Quent. It would have clarified things," Chara said huskily.

Quentin stepped away from the fireplace and reached

143

down, pulling Chara to her feet, planting a hard kiss on her mouth. "I would like nothing better than to stay here and nuzzle you, my understanding wife, but we'll be very late if I do. Shall I?"

"Don't be silly," Chara lied, wishing he would hold her forever. "We'd better go."

Quentin shrugged, quaffed the rest of his drink, then gestured for Chara to precede him.

During the drive Quentin told her about his friends the Robertses. He had attended undergraduate school with Tony and was very fond of his wife Gwen and their two little boys.

Chara listened with half an ear. Her concentration was on how to tell Quentin that she would be leaving for New York soon. She knew there would be fireworks, but she was determined to tell him tonight.

"All right, Chara, what is it now? You've hardly heard a word I've said to you. What's on your mind? Come on now, tell me. I'm not going to sit all evening and watch you bite your lip. You already need more lipstick," Quentin said, his laughter harsh when he saw her hand go unconsciously to her mouth.

Anger erupted in her at the way he could reduce her to schoolgirl status with a few words.

"If you must know, I'm going to New York at the end of the week. It's all arranged. Grinnell and I will be shooting in New York and I don't know how long I'll be gone." Chara spaced her words, glad of the anger that forced her to tell him now.

"Oh. I see." Quentin eased the powerful Ferrari around a coughing Mini, his hands seeming as strong as the car.

Chara waited in vain for the explosion, casting quick glances his way. She knew he was aware of her apprehension by the twisted smile he gave her.

"What are you waiting for, Chara? Did you think I would strangle you? I can't stop you from traveling to the

States. Would you stay here if I asked you?" Quentin's tone was offhand, as though he really didn't care what answer she gave.

"No." Chara spoke, trying to keep her voice firm. *I'd do anything for you, Quent, damn you,* Chara thought, facing away from him to look out at the beginnings of the Christmas decorations on the passing buildings.

"Well, then I saved my breath by not asking, didn't I," Quentin said mildly.

Surprisingly, the evening was pleasurable. Chara liked the Robertses and their children at once.

Robin, the lisping youngest, gave Chara a hug that brought a lump to her throat.

"Aunt Chara, you can have a baby boy and I will pway wiff him. Have it soon. I'll have some of your dwink too."

Laughing, the parents swooped down on the pajama-clad boy and carried him upstairs. David, the older boy, was already asking for a drink of water.

Chara twisted her hands together in her lap as Quentin lowered himself next to her on the settee, half-turning toward her so that his knee touched her leg. His one hand idly played with strands of her hair.

"Well, Chara, shall we have a playmate for Robin? I'm willing if you are," Quentin said offhandedly, letting his fingers tease her neck.

Wrenching away from him, Chara fought the stabbing pain that tore through her at the thought of having a little boy of Quentin's. A stocky, determined youngster of Robin's age with black curly hair and pewter-colored eyes intruded himself into Chara's mind.

Jumping to her feet, she wheeled on Quentin, still lounging on the settee, his narrowed gaze fixed on her. "You're despicable, do you know that? Making fun of something so precious . . . so beautiful. I hate you, Quent. I really do." Chara gasped, hearing the note of hysteria in her own voice.

"Calm down, Chara, Tony and Gwen will be down any moment." Quentin's cynical smile didn't hide from Chara that he was as angry as she.

In a short time Gwen and Tony were downstairs, and though Chara was sure Gwen suspected something by the searching looks she gave first to Quentin and then to her, nothing more was said between them. For the rest of the evening conversation was general, dealing with Quentin's job or hers. When they talked of the children, Chara felt that pain again, thinking of how it would be to have Quentin's child.

In the car going home the silence was oppressive. Chara looked out her side window, willing the car to go faster.

"You drank quite a bit tonight, Chara." Quentin bit off the words, his voice harsh.

"Some wine at dinner and a brandy after hardly constitutes a binge." Chara tried to match his harsh tones.

"I've told you before I don't like to see women drink too much. I don't like to see you doing it at all," Quentin rasped, jerking the car hard in a turn.

"There's too damn much about me you don't like, Mr. Perfect. Why don't you just stay away from me." Chara's reedy voice gained in strength as she turned on the seat to face him, both hands clenched.

"You little bitch," Quentin grated, striking his open hand against the steering wheel. "I'd like to . . ." Quentin growled, his jaw working as he fought his temper.

"*What?* You'd like to *what?* Hit me? Is that what you mean, you . . . you brute." Chara goaded him, wanting a physical contact with him in any way she could get it. Self-loathing made her lash out even more. "You're a hard, beastly man who would think nothing of striking a woman. That's why I hate you." Chara lied wildly, pushing the door open on her side when the car was parked. The grayish whiteness of Quentin's face seemed reinforced in the tight grooves bracketing his mouth.

Chara knew she had gone too far. With a smothered sob she made her way inside and to her bedroom, hardly aware that she undressed and climbed into bed. She felt frozen in her misery.

CHAPTER SEVEN

Chara was hardly aware of her surroundings on the entire flight from Heathrow to Kennedy. Grinnell tried a few times to engage her in conversation, but her weak replies to his overtures made him retire into a photographic magazine he had brought with him.

She felt as though her insides were being sliced with a dull blade. She missed Quentin so much she was raw with it. At the same time she was glad to be away from the cold war they had waged with each other the few days before she left. When they had met for breakfast they had been stiffly formal. Only a couple of times had they dined together. Once they had gone to a business dinner for Wainwright's. When Chara had seen Ford Talbot she had been unable to speak to him because Quentin had stayed close to her. His own attitude toward Talbot had been cold and aloof. In a way Chara had been relieved that she had been spared the explanations that she was sure Ford would have demanded of her.

When she and Quentin had parted, he had only asked if she had her key to the apartment in New York. As much as Chara would have preferred to stay anywhere else, she knew better than to try and argue the point with him. Before she could reply, he had turned from her and marched to his study, slamming the door in her face.

Her anger at him had sustained her through the taxi ride with Grinnell to the airport and for most of the flight. Now, while checking her luggage through customs, she fought the almost overwhelming sense of loss that she had experienced when she had left Quentin the first time, when she had flown from New York to London.

She dropped Grinnell at his hotel, promising that she would be at the studio that Exotica had assigned them at eight o'clock the following morning.

Suffering a slight case of jet lag, Chara yawned as she unlocked the apartment door, both eager and apprehensive about spending time there. The first thing that met her eye was the silver basket of roses sitting on the coffee table in the living room. The card with the flowers had only the letter *Q* on it. Tears pricking her eyes, Chara picked up the note lying next to the flowers. It was from Mrs. Gray, telling her that she and her husband would be in tomorrow as usual to clean, that Mr. Wainwright had informed them she was coming, that there was cold salad in the refrigerator and a banana cheesecake.

Chara looked around the empty apartment, feeling strangely comforted by the flowers and the note.

After a long, leisurely bath, Chara threw herself down on the king-size bed and fell into a long, dreamless sleep.

The first two days of her stay in the apartment were uncomfortable for Chara. Grinnell worked her hard, so that she came home dead tired. She was grateful for this because it kept the niggling reminders of Quentin from surfacing. After that Chara was able to ignore the nostalgia that being in Quentin's apartment brought up. She concentrated on her work. Grinnell was pleased.

"Chara, baby, it feels so good. This is going to be the best presentation I've ever given to Exotica. I feel it in my bones." Grinnell coughed, putting down the half-smoked cigarette and eyeing the packages she was hugging to her as she hurried in from the lunch break she had taken. "Chara, old thing, are you buying New York? Every time you come back from lunch, you're loaded down with parcels."

"New York is marvelous to shop in. I found some lovely places to buy shoes." Chara chattered, laughing as Grinnell groaned over the possible prices. Before Chara could stop him, he picked up a small bag and took a leather case out of it. Chara turned to stone as he pulled a silver chain with a miniature silver sailboat and two people hanging from it from the box. Grinnell rubbed it between his thumb and forefinger.

"That's cute the way they have the letter Q inscribed on the top of the sail and the C on the bottom. Very clever, Chara. Your husband will like it," Grinnell mused, his eyes still on the chain, so that he didn't see Chara's sudden pallor or her hands clenching at her sides. "You know, Chara, I don't like most jewelry for around a man's neck, but this is restrained, rich-looking, I think. I like it."

"Thank you. Well, we had better get to work . . ." Chara faltered, not looking at Grinnell, so that he wouldn't notice the sheen of tears in her eyes.

That night when she let herself into the apartment, the phone was ringing.

"Yes. Hello? Chara Wainwright speaking." She was a little out of breath as she eased her packages down onto the bench near the phone and unbuttoned her coat at the same time.

"Merry Christmas, Chara. How are you?" Chara felt the floor heave under her feet as she recognized her mother's voice.

"Well, aren't you going to answer me? Chara? How was the flight over? It's amazing you were able to get a seat this close to the holidays, but it will be nice for you to spend

Christmas here. New York is so classy at holiday time. Join me for dinner. Le Pavillon at eight. Bye for now." Link spoke quickly, defying interruption, her smoke-roughened voice sounding harsh.

Chara became aware that her mother had hung up when the dial tone buzzed in her ear.

She showered and dressed in a somnolent way, wishing that she could find some excuse to call off this meeting with her mother. She knew her too well not to suspect there was an ulterior motive for the dinner invitation. *No, you couldn't call it a dinner invitation,* Chara thought. It was more like a demand than an invitation. Chara didn't think for a minute that her mother had missed her. Link was a virtual stranger to the pangs of mother love.

Chara studied her slender but rounded figure in the full-length mirror in her bedroom, her nude body revolving slowly under her intense scrutiny. Without conceit, Chara knew she had a very good form, even if it was on the too-slim side. If anything, her uptilted breasts seemed emphasized by her weight loss. Two large hands could span her waist. Quent's hands, Chara thought. Her derrière was still rounded but her hips were slim. Her long legs tapered to delicate ankles and feet. She stood on tiptoe, lifting her arms high.

What a fool you are, Chara Wainwright, worrying about what your mother will say about your looks, she thought, stepping into apricot-colored silk undies. For a moment, as she studied herself in the full-length mirror, she thought of the last conversation she had had with her brother when she had called to tell him she was in England.

"Chara, don't worry about me. I'm doing fine. I love the work. I have no problems with Mother because I don't see her that much. Don't keep trying to protect me from her, Chara. I'm a big boy now. I can take care of myself," Ken had said breezily, surprising Chara, making her hope that maybe he could. "And, Chara, don't you worry about

Mother. Remember, most of the problems between you two were because you refused to grow up ugly. This call must be costing you plenty, Chara, love, so I'll say adios."

Chara blinked, bringing herself out of the reverie, smiling at the memory of her brother as she twisted her hair into the braided crown that was her trademark as the Pink Velvet Girl. As usual, she left a few pale wisps of hair curling out on her cheekbones. She sprayed herself with Joy and wriggled into a form-fitting russet silk dress that clung to her figure. The sleeves were long, with bracelet cuffs at the wrists. The neckline was high, cut straight across from shoulder tip to shoulder tip, then veeing deeply in back. Her shoes were russet leather sandals, her jacket a domestic rabbit that Quentin had assured her had been raised for eating. Chara remembered with a catch in her throat how he hadn't laughed when she told him that she couldn't wear any fur unless she knew for sure it hadn't been killed just for its coat. She recalled how he had enfolded her in his arms and told her about the rabbits.

Sighing, Chara tried to blot thoughts of him from her mind. Thinking of Quentin made her too vulnerable, and she would need all her wits about her when she was dealing with her mother.

To Chara the cab ride seemed too short. Upon entering the restaurant, she saw her mother at once. Link was sitting at a table that could easily be seen from any corner of the room.

Chara saw her mother's eyes widen, then narrow as she watched her daughter's progress across the room, her gaze touching on all the other glances on Chara.

"Chara, do sit down. That dress is a bit much, isn't it? You're making a spectacle of yourself," Link rasped, rubbing her cigarette holder between thumb and forefinger.

"You mustn't let it worry you, Mother. I'm used to it. I'm a model now, you know." Chara marveled that her voice could be so steady.

153

She avoided her mother's sudden stare by picking up the two-foot-long menu.

"Funny how you and Ken always hated show business; now you're both in it," Link purred, drawing deeply on the cigarette.

"Ken never hated it, Mother. He always wanted to get into the business. He likes his work now very much," Chara said firmly.

"Really?" Link drawled, seemingly bored by the topic. "You're too thin, Chara. Dieting can be dangerous." Link pressed her lips into a thin line.

"I don't diet, Mother. Shall we order?" Chara responded, feeling the futile anger her mother always engendered in her trying to surface.

Both women ordered steak with spinach salad on the side. Chara would have preferred swordfish, but she didn't want to precipitate her mother's annoying argument on how all fish made her nauseated.

Chara refused a cocktail, contenting herself with plain soda water and lime juice. She ignored her mother's annoyed look.

"What do you hear from Quent, Chara?" her mother shot at her, pushing a fork through her salad.

"I saw him in London. He was well," Chara answered, feeling her way, knowing that her mother would blurt out what was on her mind, given enough time.

"Umm? I understand that you don't see Kermit or Agnes anymore. Oh, don't look so suspicious. I wasn't having you watched or anything like that. Kermit called me to ask if I had intimidated you in any way to explain why you hadn't been in touch with them. He's a perfect ass, Chara, and I'm glad to see that you don't bother with that fool or his mother." Link exhaled smoke through her nose.

Chara made no retort, for once being in accord with her mother. She was looking idly around the elegant candlelit

154

restaurant, slowly chewing a bite of steak when Link spoke, her tones silky.

"When are you divorcing Quent, Chara?"

With an effort Chara kept herself from choking, finally forcing the now dry-as-dust meat down her throat. "What a question! Really, Mother, even in that loosely tied Sodom and Gomorrah you live in, marriages sometimes last a year. Mine won't be six months old until next week." Chara's smile was as brittle as her voice, she was sure, but she was determined that her mother wouldn't see how much that question hurt her.

"Come now, Chara, don't tell me you care about that marriage, because I wouldn't believe you. I don't know how you got Quent to marry you in the first place, but you can't believe that you could hold that man," Link scoffed.

"If you have invited me to dinner to interrogate me on my marriage, you have wasted your time and your money. I don't intend to discuss it and I think it would be premature of me to discuss a divorce with you, Mother, when I haven't even discussed it with Quent," Chara finished, a little breathless.

Link stared at her for long moments. Chara watched the familiar flaring of the nostrils that denoted her mother's temper was about to explode.

"Whatever it was that you wanted to say to me, Mother . . ." Chara began, her tone more placating.

"Don't you take that patronizing tone with me. You could never hold Quent's interest for long. Never. You tell him you want that divorce. I want him back in California with the production company," Link hissed, her breath rasping in anger. She seemed to erupt all at once, as though her thoughts had been slumbering like an extinct volcano that changed its mind.

Chara felt the old withdrawing as her insides shrank from the lashing confrontation she could see coming. Her own icy anger seemed to congeal her blood. Whatever her mother had in mind, Chara was determined that this time she would not be the victim or the target of her mother's vitriol. She watched her take sucking puffs on her cigarette, as though the tobacco would arm her for what was coming. Before her mother could continue, Chara pushed back her chair. "The dinner was nice, Mother, but I have no intention of trading angry insults with you. What I do with my marriage is none of your business. If you are so anxious to know about a possible divorce between Quent and myself, then I suggest that you contact him. He might tell you. I will not. Good-bye, Mother. Merry Christmas."

Link rose halfway out of her chair, as though she would stop Chara. "Why you . . . you. How dare you speak to me like that? Who the hell . . ."

While Link was still sputtering, Chara whirled in the graceful pirouette that was part of her stock-in-trade and glided to the exit, her head held high. She was unaware of the long looks cast her way. She was only intent on escaping her mother.

The cab ride was interminable. When she reached the apartment she could hardly wait to strip the clothes from her body and get into a soaking tub. She felt dirty and defiled. Her own mother's company had made her feel nauseated.

She closed her eyes and leaned against the soft tub pillow. *My God, my God,* she groaned to herself, *even I could see how much she wants Quent. My mother wants me to divorce my husband so that she can have him.* She writhed, trying to rub out her thoughts with the loofah she was clutching in her hand.

She had no sense of time as she remained in the soothing atmosphere of the bath, but when the water turned cold, she stepped, shivering, onto the bathmat. She had no recollection of drying herself; all her motions were automatic. She dropped onto her bed unclothed.

She had acquired the habit of sleeping nude in London.

She had found that it was more relaxing for her on the long nights when her mind had been filled with Quentin and sleep had been impossible.

A watery sunlight was peeping through the double-hung sheer curtains when she finally turned over in sleep, promising herself that she would make an effort to have a Christmas party even if it would only be Grinnell and herself. Perhaps it was that optimistic thought that allowed her to sleep.

Grinnell's habitual placidity was ruffled by Chara's pallor and the dark smudges under her eyes.

"Chara, for God's sake, what are you doing to yourself? You look like you sell coffins for a living. Have you been partying it up or what?" he growled, concern lacing through his irritation.

"Partying?" Chara asked harshly, her eyebrows arching. "I would hardly call it partying. Oh, never mind. Let me put some other makeup on. Maybe I can cover up the shadows." Chara shrugged, about to turn away.

"Wait, love. Tell old Grinnell what's the matter. Is it that husband of yours? Something is eating away at you." Grinnell gave a twisted smile. "It's not just the job that's worrying me, Chara. I . . . I hate to see you so unhappy. I'm a good listener, if you want to talk about it."

Chara didn't want to talk about Link. She didn't even want to think about her, but she knew that he wouldn't be fobbed off with any lame excuse.

"It's my mother, Grinnell. She's making demands of me that I cannot meet: It kept me awake most of the night thinking about what she said to me over dinner. She's a very high-pressure lady." Chara smiled weakly, knowing she could never mention to anyone the content of her conversation with her mother.

"I've heard of Meta Lincoln Styles, Chara. Don't look so surprised that I should know about her. Some of those photographers in Hollywood are friends of mine. One,

Charlie Davis, was head cameraman on a movie made from your mother's book. He told me no one could keep her in order but your husband. She had a mouth like an M-1, Charlie said. Not that I want to run down your mother, Chara, but that's what he said," Grinnell explained.

"I know you're not trying to run her down, Grinnell. Don't worry, I have no illusions about my mother. She's a very hard lady to deal with." Chara grimaced.

"Then maybe you had better let your husband handle her." Grinnell laughed, stamping out his cigarette. Chara was glad he was looking at the ashtray. She had the feeling that all the pain that was tearing her up inside was showing in her face. She hurried away to touch up her makeup.

Shooting didn't go well in spite of Chara's determination and Grinnell's placatory manner. Chara was glad when he called a halt.

It was while she was changing into street clothes that she remembered the promise she had made to herself just before she had gone to sleep the night before.

"Grinnell." Chara approached the desk where the photographer was scrutinizing some negatives.

"Umm, what is it, Chara?"

"Well, Christmas is coming and I thought I would like to have a party at my apartment. It probably wouldn't be big since I really don't know anyone in New York, but I thought that you and I . . ." Chara shrugged, looking at him as he straightened away from the desk.

"Hey, that doesn't sound half bad. I have a few friends in this city that I could ask, and let's not forget the people at Exotica." Grinnell nodded his head as he ticked off names on his fingers.

Chara named the twenty-third of December as a good day because it was a Saturday—and it was her six-month anniversary. She would have something that would blot out the thoughts of Quentin for the entire evening.

"Why don't I come over some evening to your flat and help you decorate, Chara?" Grinnell asked, beaming.

Chara slapped a surprised hand to her cheek. "Oh, Lord, I didn't even think of decorations. I'll have to ask Quent's day couple if there are any old ones that I could use. The rest I'll buy."

Grinnell seemed to warm to the subject the more they discussed the party. He even allowed that it might be all right for Chara to come in late the following day so that she might speak with the day help when they arrived.

The next day Chara poked around the apartment on her own while waiting for the couple to arrive. She wandered into Quentin's study on her return from the pantry, where she had tried every cupboard and drawer but had found no Christmas decorations.

She felt his presence deeply in the totally masculine room dominated by oak paneling and a marble fireplace. Unlike the rest of the very modern apartment, this room had a traditional English look.

About to turn away and leave the room, Chara noticed a picture frame sitting prominently on the desk so that anyone sitting in the big chair would be looking right at the picture itself. Chara ambled around the desk, curious to see what or who had the place of honor right under Quentin's eye.

Her gasp was loud in the stillness as she looked at the picture of herself and Gulliver laughing on the beach at Cayuga Lake.

Chara remembered seeing the picture when Quentin had picked up the printed roll at the local drugstore. At the time she had made a comment that it looked as though she and Gulliver were appreciating the same joke. The dog's mouth was open, with his tongue lolling to one side and all his impressive incisors showing. Quentin had agreed that the dog was laughing.

Chara wondered when he had had the enlargement

made. A rattling at the outer door interrupted her thoughts, and she left the study, pulling the door closed behind her.

She went forward to meet the two open-mouthed persons standing in the foyer, putting out her hand first to the woman, then to the man.

"How do you do. I'm Mrs. Wainwright. I know we've never done more than exchange notes, but I feel that I know you both. You do such a wonderful job with the apartment."

"I'm Mrs. Cross, ma'am, and this is my husband, Jake. Thank you for saying them nice words. It was nice of Mrs. Wainwright, wasn't it, Jake?"

"Yep," Jake replied.

Chara smiled at the taciturn Jake, then turned back to Mrs. Cross and asked about the Christmas decorations.

It seemed to take no time before an assortment of holiday paraphernalia was in the foyer. Chara was enthusiastic about most of the things but absolutely refused to allow Jake to set up the plastic Christmas tree, insisting that she would buy a real one and decorate it.

A happy Chara staggered into Grinnell's studio close to the lunch hour, dragging a bushy evergreen behind her.

"What the hell are you doing, Chara? What is that?" Grinnell growled, trying to rescue one of his precious tripods that teetered precariously as Chara pushed by.

"A balsam," she answered, sighing, sinking into the nearest chair and removing her boots. "The man assured me that it was very fresh. Take hold of a branch and squeeze, Grinnell. Nothing smells more like Christmas to me than the smell of balsam. Now I have a whole beautiful tree just oozing that beautiful smell." Chara beamed beatifically when Grinnell snorted.

"How are you going to get that home, may I ask?" Grinnell pointed his cigarette at the offending tree that was now taking up a good share of his studio.

"Cab." Chara assured him, not at all put out when he guffawed with derision, telling her that no taxi driver in all of Manhattan would take that monster into his cab. Chara raised a disdainful eyebrow and insisted she would have no trouble.

A while later she was wishing she had bet with Grinnell on the outcome of whether she would get a cab or not. Not only did her cabbie help her load it into the car but he sang Christmas songs with Chara all the way to the apartment, then helped her get her tree into the lobby. Chara gave him a ten-dollar tip and wished him a happy holiday.

The struggle in the elevator was more than she had bargained for, but she was finally able to press the button so that she and her tree sped up to their floor.

Panting and pulling, she managed to get the tree from the elevator to the door.

After finally balancing the tree against the wall, she inserted her key. Before she could turn it, the door opened. She looked up, open-mouthed.

"Hello, little bride, can I help you with that?" Quentin drawled.

CHAPTER EIGHT

Staggering, Chara fell against him. Before she could pull away, he had wrapped her in his arms and pressed his open mouth to hers. The familiar languor overcame her. Despite her wrathful warnings to herself, she pressed closer to him, her arms reaching around his waist. Quentin lifted his head fractionally, letting his liquid silver eyes rove the face so close to him.

"Miss me? Your mouth looks delicious, love, but your little nose is red with cold," Quentin whispered, seemingly not aware they were standing in the hall, his fingers threading through her hair.

"My nose always gets red in the cold," Chara mumbled, squirming out of his grasp. She tried not to look at the satirical smile on those sensuous lips of his, but she found it hard not to look at him.

"What have we here?" Quentin sighed, straightening away from her.

"It's a Christmas tree." Chara smiled shyly. "Do you mind that I bought a real one, Quent? There was a plastic one, but I can't abide them. Of course, if you don't want this in your apartment—"

"*Our* apartment, wife, yours and mine. It so happens that I like real trees myself, but it's been so long since I really took a hand in the Christmas decorating." Quentin shrugged, ushering her in before tackling the balsam himself. "Where would you like this unwieldy thing, love?"

Chara didn't answer for a moment. She just stood, hands clasped, looking at her purchase. "Isn't it beautiful, Quent? We have lights and ever so many beautiful ornaments. Some of them are very old."

"Yes, Chara, I get the picture." Quent staggered. "Now where would you like this? Unless you'd like me just to stand here through New Year's Day balancing this evergreen bear. Wasn't there a smaller one?" He groaned as Chara giggled and gestured to him to follow her into the sitting room.

With a flourish she pointed to a spot in front of the sliding glass doors leading to the terrace. The outdoor garden was now filled with snow.

"Won't it be beautiful here, Quent? In the daytime it will have the backdrop of snow on the terrace. At night the lights will be reflected in the glass." Chara beamed at Quentin's smile. "Oh, I'm sorry. You'll want the stand, won't you? Wait right there, I'll get it." Chara yelped, sprinting to the hall and rifling through a large carton sitting there.

When she returned, Quentin had propped the tree against the glass door, balancing it with one hand, watching her galloping return with amusement.

"I hope you had planned to let Jake set this up for you and decorate it, Chara," Quentin drawled, showing her how to steady it while he tried to fit it in the holder. "Because you sure couldn't have handled it yourself. Hold it tight now, Chara, I have to get a saw. The trunk of this thing is too thick. I'll have to whittle the bottom. Can you hold it by yourself?" Quentin half-laughed as she assured him that she could and that she would have had no trouble decorating it herself. She shouted this last part because Quentin had departed to find the tools he needed. When he returned, he stood there in the doorway, amusement lighting his face, making him look years younger.

Flushed and struggling, Chara glared at him. "Well, don't just stand there. I'm getting hot standing around in my coat. I know you, you're just paying me back for making you hold the tree." Chara panted.

"Exactly, lovely one." Quentin laughed, taking the tree from her so that she could remove her coat. "Come on now, Chara, stop glaring at me and pull the tree your way. That's it."

Chara was horrified that Quentin was going to saw the tree right on their beautiful carpet, but before she could say anything he had begun.

When they finally finished and Chara had vacuumed up the shavings and the few needles that the tree had shed, both she and Quentin stepped back to observe their handiwork.

Quentin put his arm around her waist, his fingers massaging her narrow middle.

He had no idea how he was affecting her, Chara told herself irritably. How he'd laugh if he knew she wanted to wrap herself around him and stay that way forever. Chara wished she had the strength of character to pull away from him, but it felt so good to have him near her, touching her.

"It is a beautiful tree, little wife. Perhaps some philistine might think it's too much for just the two of us, but I don't, do you?" Quentin whispered, his breath fanning Chara's forehead.

Chara stepped away from him, feeling his hard-eyed stare on her at once. "Well, you see, Quent, it's not just for the two of us." Chara cleared her throat.

"No?" Quentin's voice was cool.

"No." Chara swallowed. "I . . . I thought I was going to be alone, so I decided to have a party on Saturday."

"Our six-month anniversary in fact," Quentin said.

Chara's head swung around, making her hair fly across her cheek. "You remembered?" she said incredulously, then had the grace to blush at his satiric smile. "What I mean is I didn't think you would remember and I thought—" Chara paused.

"What did you think, Chara? I was there at your side six months ago. Do you remember that? I can't forget it," Quentin averred, his voice harsh.

Chara turned away quickly so he wouldn't see the tears in her eyes. Her mother was right. Quentin hated being married to her. He did want a divorce. Chara geared herself to say something about getting one when Quentin stepped behind her and took hold of her shoulders.

"All right, Chara, we'll have a party. I really should anyway. I'll call a few of my friends if it's all right with you. I'm sure they'll stop by. Is that all right with you?" Quentin asked, his lips just touching the nape of her neck for a moment.

Chara could barely control the tremor that ran through her at his touch. She could only hope he hadn't noticed as she nodded her head in answer to his question.

Quentin left her, saying that he was going to shower. Chara nodded again without turning her head.

She stared unseeingly at the large balsam, wondering how she was going to remain in his company for any length of time without betraying herself to him. God, how she hated the hold he had over her! No, she loved it. There was no going back for her. She would love Quentin forever. He was the only man she wanted to love her. Shaking hands massaged her cheeks as she wondered if she should broach the subject of divorce before he did. She paced in a small area in front of the tree but found no answer, except that she knew she couldn't face asking Quentin for a divorce. She pictured in her mind a gleeful Quentin, delighting in the thought of being free of her. No, she would wait until he asked, then she would capitulate.

A Pyrrhic victory! She sighed and went out to the hall and began to lug the cartons of ornaments into the living room.

She had strings of lights stretched out on the rug. One by one she tested the strings and was pleased to find that she would need only three replacement bulbs. She sat back on her heels, biting her lip, realizing that for such a big tree she would need at least four or five more sets of lights.

Quentin came downstairs, his hair slightly damp, wearing an open-necked, longsleeved shirt in a deep cream color and dark brown velvet jeans that hugged his muscular calves and thighs.

Chara felt dry mouthed as she looked at him. She took a deep breath and turned away, struggling into her coat.

"Where are you going, love?" Quentin asked, his voice low and vibrant.

Chara explained about the lack of lights and how she was going to take a cab downtown and pick up some more.

Quentin told her it was a good idea and said that he would come with her. He laughed at Chara when she told him stiff-lipped that she wouldn't let him leave the apartment until his hair was dry, then sprinted up the stairs to get her hair dryer.

She was staggered when Quentin submitted docilely to her demands that he sit still while she blew-dry his hair. Chara would never have believed that she would have such undiluted pleasure from drying a man's hair. Quentin responded beautifully to Chara's ministrations, and her fingers found undisguised joy in the crisp, black wiriness.

"Are you satisfied now, little bride? Let me get my jacket, then we'll go." Quentin smiled at her, rising from his chair, and hugged her to him before she could step back. Then he pressed a light kiss to her mouth.

Dazed, Chara followed him down to the cab procured by the doorman, then allowed herself to be caught close to Quentin in the wild taxi ride.

"Do you know, since I've met you, Chara, I've really come to like a Manhattan cab ride," Quentin whispered in her hair, amusement threading his voice. "You belong cuddled up to me, little bride, and I enjoy it."

Chara gulped, knowing she should move away from him but unable to deny herself the wonderful feel of his arms around her. She gave a sigh and snuggled closer.

When she and Quentin wended their way through the happy holiday throng, Chara didn't demur when Quentin clasped her hand. The department store was mobbed with last-minute shoppers, but Chara blessed them, sure in her own mind that Quentin wouldn't be holding her hand unless there was a mob of people.

She and Quentin took the escalator to the second floor of the department store and were guided by a floorwalker to the right section. They had no trouble getting the lights, but Chara was drawn to the large display of ornaments. She couldn't make up her mind what to buy.

"Love, why don't you take your time. I have a little shopping to finish, so why don't I meet you back here in—" Quentin glanced quickly at his white-gold wristwatch "—say in an hour. Will that suit you?"

Chara nodded, trying to smile but wanting to tell him that she didn't want to be separated from him for an hour.

In that hour Chara was able to settle on her choice of ornaments, then she was able to buy a book on sailing for Quentin's nephew, Dennis, a tiny flacon of perfume for Amy, a silk scarf for Clem, and a meerschaum pipe for Jack.

When Quentin returned to her a little late, his raised eyebrow asked what all the packages were. She laughed as he tried to keep his balance with the two unwieldly bags he took from Chara plus his own parcels.

"I've told you what I bought, Quent. Now tell me what you purchased," Chara demanded, guiding him toward the exit.

"No." Quentin struggled. "I'm not going to tell you anything. Little girls shouldn't be nosy or Santa Claus won't come." Quentin bit off the words, his brooding gaze aloof from Chara.

What has set him off this time? Chara asked herself, puzzled and irritated by his lightning spin into a black mood. She was half-running, trying to keep up with his long-legged stride, barely impeded by the load of packages he was toting.

"Won't it be hard to get a cab in all this crowd, Quent?" she asked, panting a little, wanting to punch him in the nose for ignoring her.

"No. I told our cabbie to check on us every hour in front of the store. For fifty bucks he was willing. Hurry up," he barked.

Chara felt deflated; the brightness had gone from the day. She wished with all her heart that Quentin had stayed in England. Damn him for making everything plastic and uninteresting. Damn him!

Chara was glad in the next few days that plans for the party took up all her free time. She and Quentin were like coldly polite strangers when they were together. Many times Chara could feel her fingernails digging into her palms. She itched to claw and tear at him. She was appalled at the depth of the violence she felt toward him. It didn't mitigate her feelings one iota. She could have cheerfully broken his nose, loosened all his teeth with a claw hammer, and blackened his eyes with a brick. She wanted to tap his kneecap with a club.

On the day of the party Quentin was gone before she arose. Then to her chagrin Grinnell kept her late. One of his helper's had destroyed almost a complete day's shooting because of a mistake in developing time.

"Chara, baby, I'm sorry, but I had to have those pictures. I know the party's tonight, but you have to give me the time," he pleaded.

"Yes, all right, I'll come in." Chara sighed, mentally revising her list of things to do.

Chara scrambled into her clothes and scribbled down items that she wanted the day help to accomplish before she arrived home. The cryptic note she left Quentin just said that she would be back early in the afternoon hopefully.

At three o'clock a repentant Grinnell told her they were done. Weary to her bones, Chara glared at him.

"I know, baby." Grinnell shrugged, squinting around the smoke from his cigarette. "It's been a grind of a session, but I had to finish. Look, let me come by early and give you a hand. All right?"

Chara smiled at the elfin regret on his face, nodding. "I don't know why I put up with you. You're a slavedriver. Come at about ten minutes to seven. You can take coats. Don't bother showing me out, Simon Legree." Chara gave a wide yawn. "I'm going home and have a nap."

As Chara was leaving, Grinnell called after her.

"By the way, Chara, I was down at the Exotica offices and ran into Ford Talbot. I invited him to the party, all right?" Grinnell asked.

Chara nodded, then left, rubbing at the frown she could feel on her forehead with her free hand. She hoped Quentin wouldn't be even more difficult when he saw Ford at the party, but what could she do, she argued with herself.

Adding to her temper was her inability to flag a taxi. Hitching her makeup and clothing carryall higher on her shoulder, she started walking. Twice she was splashed with slush as she crossed intersections. Two blocks from the apartment a cab stopped. She was so tired she took it.

Blindly she let herself into the apartment, not even

going toward the activity she could hear in the living room. Instead she went right to her room, shed her clothes, and lowered herself into a steaming, scented tub. She lay there unmoving until the water started to cool, then shampooed her head and rinsed it with the long spray-head-ended hose that she attached to the tub faucet. She had a bath fetish, she thought hazily.

Chara draped a soft towel over her and wrapped another turbanlike around her head. She polished her nails, then dried and fluffed her hair. Hardly able to keep her eyes open, she climbed naked between her silk sheets and was asleep at once.

When she half-woke an hour later, she felt strong hands caressing her body, urging her up. Relaxed and warm, her eyes still closed, she reached up and dug her hands into strong muscular shoulders, loving the feel of the skin. The body sank down on hers and she purred with satisfaction.

"Unless you would like me to call off this party while I kiss you from head to toe, you should start getting ready. Our guests will be here in half an hour," Quentin growled into her ear. "Of course I'd rather be stroking you, little kitten."

Quentin's mouth roved over her body, lingering at her breasts. His mouth brushed from one rosy lip to the other. Chara could feel heat spreading through her body as her fingers touched his skin, her fingers pulling at the curly hairs on his chest. She sighed, lifting her eyelids to look at his face.

The cold twist to his mouth didn't match his low voice. Chara felt the languorous heat in her blood cool as she looked into those silver marble eyes.

"You had better leave so that I can dress, Quent," Chara said, glad that her cool tones didn't show the turmoil inside her. She felt his hands dig into her flesh, a flare of anger giving his eyes a liquid sheen.

171

Then he rolled away from her and off the bed to his feet in one fluid motion. He turned to give her one last derisive glance that went the length of her body.

"Even a little too slim you have a delectable form, little bride. I was always a man who appreciated art," he said insolently before swift strides took him to the door.

Almost sobbing with anger, Chara threw the pillows one after the other at the closing door.

"Where the hell does he get off talking to me that way, treating me like I'm some . . . some . . . oh, I don't know . . ." Chara hissed to her image in the mirror as she tried for the third time to put on a sapphire drop earring.

Amazed that her makeup was flawless after applying it with unsteady hands, she studied her skin, noting that the pearly blue eyeshadow deepened the color of her eyes. She stood and twirled in front of the full-length mirror, liking the satiny feel of the midnight blue silk dress that swathed her figure to the calf, then flared at the bottom to a cascade of ruffles, higher in front than in back. It was strapless and very sexy. Chara had a moment of misgiving, then lifted her chin. Her model's figure and the sleek crown of her hair gave her courage. She was about to fasten the necklace of sapphires Quentin had given her that matched the earrings when she decided that the bareness of her throat and shoulders was more dramatic.

"Lovely. You're lovely, Chara, but dangerous in that dress," Quentin drawled.

Chara whirled away from the mirror, wondering how long he had been standing there. Before she could speak, he held out a jeweler's box.

"Happy six-month anniversary, little bride. I think you'll find that you can wear this with your dress." He spoke, his tones expressionless, his face the same.

Chara looked at the perfect pearl with the slight bluish cast to it, then back at Quentin.

"Don't look so wary, Chara. It's normal for a man to

172

give his wife gifts on their anniversary." He laughed harshly, taking the ring from the box and fitting it to the third finger of her right hand.

She didn't say that she thought it unusual for a man to give his wife a six-month-anniversary gift if he was going to divorce her soon. She thought it but didn't say it. She didn't want Quentin thinking along those lines. Besides, they weren't arguing, they were standing close to one another. With grim determination Chara clutched at the moment as one more treasure she could store up against the time they would be parted. She wouldn't think of that, of never seeing Quentin again.

"Do you like it, Chara?" Quentin rasped. Chara raised her hand, twisting it this way and that. Those silver eyes lifted to her face, probing each pore as though her face were a code he was breaking.

I would like anything you gave me, she wanted to scream at him. *I would like it if you gave me nothing, if only you wouldn't leave me.* She kept her eyes on the ring, not wanting him to read her thoughts. She'd be damned if she would help him decode her mind. "Yes. I like it very much, Quent," she answered coolly. "But I think we should go downstairs. It's time to greet our guests."

"They'll be here soon, yes, but not yet. I want my gift from you first," he said roughly, hauling her into his arms, his mouth imprisoning her. She struggled at first. Then a feeling of weakness took her. Her arms lifted to clasp his neck, her hands raking through his thick, crisp hair.

Quentin felt her submit and grasped her closer, his mouth moving from her mouth to her throat, then down to a shoulder.

"Are you going to be angry with me for smearing your makeup?" Quentin laughed in her ear, his voice husky and unsteady.

"No, Exotica assures me that their makeup is smear-proof," Chara answered idly, her hands stroking his neck.

173

"Good. I knew that there had to be something about that outfit that I didn't despise," he hissed, anger in his voice.

Chara tried to lean back to look at him, wondering at the remark, but he covered her mouth with his again and Chara forgot everything.

The ring of the doorbell levered them apart.

Quentin lifted his head slowly, one finger stroking her cheek, staring at her for a moment. Then he left the room.

Chara's hands were shaking as she applied a little fresh lipgloss. As her right hand came up to her face, the soft pinkish gleam of the pearl caught her gaze. She stared at it for long seconds, knowing that this would be a difficult task for her, returning the ring to Quentin when they parted. Taking a deep breath, she touched the ring, then left the room to descend the stairs to the hall.

Quentin was talking to Grinnell and another man who was shrugging out of his overcoat. Turning, the man looked straight up the stairs at her.

"Hello, Chara. You look lovely. Happy Christmas."

"Merry Christmas, Ford. It's nice to see you," Chara said, not daring to look at Quentin, feeling his burning anger scald her as Ford came forward and kissed her gently.

CHAPTER NINE

Chara could feel Quentin's eyes on her wherever she moved. To her surprise, she didn't feel uncomfortable under that scrutiny. She was intensely aware of him, but it seemed to make her more alert, more responsive to her guests. She glided from group to group, more at ease than she had ever been in her life. She knew from the admiring stares of the men and the assessing glances of the women that she looked her best. That, plus the vibrations between Quentin and herself, were far more stimulating to her than alcohol could ever be. As usual, Chara contented herself with Perrier and lime, not wanting to court the headache that alcohol could give her.

When Chara saw her mother wending her way toward her through clusters of people, she stiffened, resentment riding hard on her. Quentin invited her, Chara thought. Her fingernails dug into her palms as she thought this. She braced herself against her mother's first words.

"Hello, darling, nice party. You do spend Quent's money, don't you?" Link purred, stabbing the air with her ridiculously long cigarette holder. "Perhaps you should have called me and I could have helped you with this bash," Link said, looking around the room in a bored way, her smoke-harshened voice grating on Chara's nerves.

The hard arm encircling her waist startled Chara. When she would have pulled free, Quentin's grip tightened in painful deliberation. He looked dangerous, a mirthless twist to his mouth, his eyes agate hard. "Has everyone here told you how lovely you are, my sweet? Each time I look for you, I find you surrounded by admiring men," he purred. Lifting his eyes from her, he turned to look at her mother.

"How are you, Link? I hear through the grapevine that you've been asking for me. What's the problem?" Quentin drawled, his one hand at Chara's waist beginning to move in sensuous rhythm on her hip.

Without answering Quentin, Link's eyes were drawn to the motion of his hand. Then she looked up pointedly at Chara. Without thinking, Chara began to withdraw from Quentin's hold but he pulled her tighter to his side.

Lips tightening in anger, Link twirled the cigarette holder, letting the ash fall to the carpet. "Perhaps it would be better if we talked more privately, Quent. Let's say somewhere less distracting, like my hotel. I'll be staying until the day after Christmas so . . ."

"Sorry, Link, no dice. Chara and I will be leaving for upstate tomorrow. If the weather stays fair, Ken will be joining us. We're going to have Christmas dinner with my family. Then we'll be staying on for a while. My plans are up in the air after that. Get in touch with Judson. He can deal with any problem you might have," Quentin stated, his voice cold.

Chara drew a deep breath at the hard-eyed animosity Link was leveling at her husband, but Quentin seemed impervious as he turned Chara without another word to introduce her to friends of his. "This is Brad Tilby, darling, from Boston. We were roommates in college. That's his wife just walking toward us now. Bea, Bea, come here

176

and let me introduce you to my wife." Quentin bent down and kissed the diminutive, obviously Latin lady. "Remember your beautiful lace shawl you love so much? Well, it was Bea's grandmother who made that for you. Contesa Louisa makes her home in New York. Beatriz Maria Elena Vinceiro attended Radcliffe when Brad and I were at Harvard. It was love at first sight, but he stole her from me." Quentin laughed as Bea pouted at the compliment, kissing Quentin's jaw, then turning to Chara. "So you're Chara: At last we're meeting you, after hearing nothing but your name from Quentin's lips for months," tiny, dark-eyed Bea trilled, grasping Chara's right hand with her own. "My God, Q, she's a beauty . . . so young too."

Chara felt Quentin grip her body in a convulsive movement. Then Brad Tilby was in front of her, trying to pry her from Quentin's hold as he bent over and gave her a big kiss. Chara looked up into his twinkling brown eyes and giggled as he pushed at Quentin.

"Let go of her, will you, Q? My God, old son, I knew if you went down, you'd take a hard fall, but I didn't expect you to be pole-axed." Brad's Yankee twang cut through the loud music that someone had turned too high. He looked down at Chara, a pixie smile on his big, rugged face. "He described you to me and I thought he must be exaggerating No one could be that great. He was right. You are."

Chara stared at Brad in wonder, then turned to look at Quentin. Two coin-sized spots of red colored his cheekbones. He didn't look at her.

"Don't pay any attention to these two, Chara. They're trouble from start to finish," Quentin averred, the twist to his lips even more pronounced. "Try not to believe anything they say about me."

"Monster," Bea chortled, kissing Quentin on the chin again, then turning to Chara. "He was a heartthrob even in college, Chara. Old Love 'Em and Leave 'Em Wainwright, they used to call him. He never changed until he met you." Bea's laughter increased when Quentin shook her playfully.

He didn't change then, Chara thought to herself, catching another assessing glance that a curvaceous blonde sent toward Quentin as she passed in the arm of a Wainwright executive. Quentin returned the look with a head-to-toe look of his own. Chara hated his smile.

Chara heard Bea make a sound of disgust and turned to look at her. The other woman's gaze was directed toward the doorway of the living room.

"Oh, Lord, who invited her?" Bea hissed, moving closer to Chara as the two men spoke to a passing acquaintance.

"Who is it?" Chara whispered, watching the statuesque auburn-haired beauty who stood poised in the doorway, scanning the room, fully aware of the many eyes on her.

"That, my dear Chara, is our own twentieth-century Jezebel, Zina Prentiss, star of stage, cinema, and bedroom," Bea answered, bitterness lacing her voice. She looked at Chara wryly. "Oh, yes, she had her hooks into Brad for a time and I was scared to death. I thought sure . . . well, anyway, we survived it and we're closer than we ever were, but that woman is a barracuda." She sighed, looking at Chara. "I don't know why I'm telling you this on such short acquaintance, but I feel that you're a friend already."

"I feel the same, Bea. Whoops. Don't look now, but I think the barracuda is swimming this way." Chara gave a little laugh that choked off at Bea's next words.

"I'm not surprised. She's spotted Quent. He's the only man she could never whistle to heel and she has tried. Boy, has she tried. She tracks him down wherever he is." Bea stared at the woman sailing toward them. She didn't see the stricken look on Chara's face or how her hands clenched when Zina threw herself into Quentin's arms and kissed him full on the mouth.

"Darling," Zina caroled. "It's been ever so long. Aren't you going to wish me Merry Christmas? Brad, how nice . . . and your lovely wife, eh, Barbie." Zina shrugged, not listening when Brad corrected her on Bea's name. Instead she wound her perfectly manicured hands through Quentin's arm, pouting up at him. Quentin's lips lifted in a cynical smile as he covered her one hand with one of his.

"How are you, Zina? I haven't seen you in a while," he drawled, suddenly looking up at a white-faced Chara. "Let me introduce you to my wife. Darling, this is Zina Prentiss, the actress. Zina, this is my wife, Chara Wainwright." Quentin's lips lifted in a smile that didn't reach his eyes. Chara noticed he didn't move away from the barracuda.

She could feel tongues of fiery anger lashing through her. She felt like dumping her glass of champagne over his head. *Wouldn't you think he would uncoil himself from that woman,* Chara grated to herself. Swallowing bile, she put out her hand and mumbled a greeting. When the other woman ignored her hand and just looked her over blankly from head to foot, Chara's chin came out. She took a deep breath and excused herself, saying that she had to see to her other guests.

Blindly she turned away, sighting Grinnell near the grand piano. She headed straight for him, as though she wanted nothing more than to join the singing throng around the piano.

"It's a great party, Chara. I didn't think we would have this many people. There are more famous people here this evening than I ever saw in all my years in London. It's great," Grinnell crowed, a rosy glow on his features that owed much to the champagne punch that he seemed to enjoy so much.

"Yes, it is a good party," Chara echoed, her voice hollow. She was glad the photographer was a trifle high, so that he wouldn't notice how miserable she was. She

179

watched him as he craned his neck to look around her as a full-blown redhead glided by. She had to smile at his wide-eyed appreciation. His eyes were still on the redhead when he spoke to her.

"Chara, I was talking to your mother. She said there was always a need for good still photographers in California. Do you think I should try my luck out there when my contract with Exotica runs out?" Grinnell muttered, sipping his punch but watching the redhead. "You know, I'm quite happy I ran into her at the Exotica office the other day, otherwise she mightn't have known about our party. She seemed pretty pleased when I told her about it. I knew you would want her to come, even if you've had some differences with her." Grinnell looked back to Chara, his slightly tipsy smile elfin in appeal.

Chara stared at him long moments without answering. "Are you saying that it was you who invited my mother here this evening?" Chara breathed loudly.

"Yes. I saw her at Wainwright's one morning when I took some proofs in to Mac Webster." Grinnell nodded, smiling. "Well, what do you think, Chara? Should I try my hand in California?"

"Umm . . . ah . . . what? California? Ah, no. I really don't think I'd chance it. If you had a firm commitment from an outfit out there, yes, but I think it would be more to your advantage to try to get your contract renewed with Exotica," Chara answered earnestly, trying hard to concentrate on what she was saying to Grinnell.

"Thanks, Chara." Grinnell beamed at her, his eyes getting a glassy tinge. Chara wondered if he would even remember their conversation in the morning. He looked up, focusing on something over Chara's shoulder. "Oh, hi there, Ford. Good party, isn't it?"

Ford nodded and smiled at Grinnell, then turned to Chara. "Dance with me, lovely Pink Velvet Girl?"

"Of course I'll dance with you, Ford." Chara tried to

smile at him as she entered his arms, keeping her eyes from the corner where Quentin was in close conversation with the striking Zina Prentiss. She spotted her mother making her determined way to that laughing corner. *They deserve each other,* Chara thought nastily. *Let them bleed to death from the tongue lacerations they'll give one another. And I hope Zina Prentiss gets caught in the fallout.* She shut her eyes resolutely as Ford pressed her closer, whirling her through the living room door to the relative quiet of the foyer. He stopped her all at once and leaned back a little.

"At last I have you where I want you, said the spider to the fly." Ford leered at Chara, then glanced upward at the mistletoe.

Before Chara could do anything but gasp in laughter, Ford had swooped down, his mouth clamping tight to hers. Chara found the sensation pleasant but not exciting. She did nothing to free herself even as Ford tightened his hold and whispered her name against her mouth.

Her eyes flew open as she felt herself lifted roughly and Ford thrust away from her.

Quentin was standing there, his dark good looks satanic in his anger. She could almost see the crackling fires of Hades in his hot, silver eyes. Mute, Chara's heart beat fiercely against her chest wall as she watched Quentin's hands lift like talons when he went for Ford. She looked at him with unbelieving eyes, mesmerized by his monumental rage.

Before he reached Ford, Grinnell and Brad were in front of him, each one of them holding an arm. Chara was sure they wouldn't be able to hold him, as his strength was carrying the two men backward as he struggled toward the waiting, cold-eyed Ford.

Coming out of her horrified trance, Chara went to Ford, urging him to leave, keeping her voice low.

"Get the hell away from him, Chara," Quentin grated,

181

straining against the other two men. "You bastard, get away from my wife."

"Go, Ford, please, go now," Chara pleaded, her back to the thrashing Quentin.

"I don't thank you for the interference, Chara. I would have loved the chance to smash your husband's mouth," Ford said coldly, shrugging her arm away and heading for the door.

"Not as much as I want to smash yours, and I will if you ever come near her again," Quentin said through his teeth.

The door slammed shut behind Ford. In the sudden silence Chara looked around her, surprised that none of the other guests had seemed to notice the commotion. For the first time that evening she was glad that the stereo had been turned too high.

At Quentin's growled imprecation, she looked around at the three men clustered together as the two released him. Grinnell seemed cold sober. Brad was shaking his head and trying to straighten his tie. Quentin just stood there, body forward, his hands hanging loose, staring at Chara.

"Whew, old man, I haven't seen you like this since we lost in rowing to the Yalies, but then you were roaring drunk. I'd forgotten what a temper you have. Chara, are you all right?" Brad asked, a rueful smile on his face.

"Yes, I'm fine," Chara murmured, her own anger and humiliation at Quentin's antics boiling deep inside of her.

Grinnell put his arm around Brad's shoulders and steered him toward the living room. "Come with me. I'll buy you a drink. You're a good man in a brawl. I can see that."

"You're not so bad yourself, Grinnell," Brad chortled. With a last narrow-eyed look from Chara to Quentin, he allowed himself to be led away.

"How dare you do such a thing," Chara whispered, her voice throbbing in anger.

Quentin's head swung as though on a pendulum. To Chara's bemused mind he looked like a prizefighter coming out of his corner. His eyes leaped with the same murderous rage she had seen in them when he had looked at Ford.

"You had no right," Chara said, confused.

"No right? You little bitch. Who has a better right? You're my wife, Chara. You think I'm going to just stand by and let that bastard take my wife. Think again," Quentin growled, his mouth working, his voice thickened with strong emotion. His hard lips ground together as though the thought were too much to handle.

"You fondle and hang over the lovely Zina and expect me to like it. Then when a friend kisses me under the mistletoe you hit the ceiling like a jealous maniac. What kind of double standard do you operate under, Quent? Whatever it is, it isn't my standard and—" Chara subsided when a hoarse voice intruded.

"What's this? Trouble in paradise?" Link husked, drawing deep on her stiletto-length cigarette holder, a malicious smile lighting her features.

"Get out of here, Link," Quentin growled, never taking his eyes from Chara. "I don't care if you are her mother, this is none of your business. What Chara and I have to say to each other is no concern of yours. Do I have to repeat myself? Leave us alone. By the way, before you leave tonight, wish your daughter a Merry Christmas. We're flying up to our place tomorrow to have Christmas with my sister and her family. We won't be back for a while."

Chara stared at him, at a loss for words. Her heart started to beat in heavy cadence at the thought of being at the lake and she stiffened as she thought of Zina Prentiss. She bit an already tense lip and turned away, mumbling something about going to the powder room.

When she returned downstairs, some of the guests were beginning to leave. Quentin was standing with them, now at ease. Chara looked at him dumbfounded. The scene with Ford might never have taken place.

"Oh, here you are, darling—the Chamberses are leaving." Quentin turned to her, the smile back in place, his eyes showing their usual coldness. He snaked an arm around Chara's waist, holding her close to him.

When they returned to the living room, he didn't release her, but steered her over to the piano where Bea was playing some college drinking songs that she assured Chara had fifty verses each.

"Each of these is racier than the other, Chara, and I wouldn't think of playing any of them, except that most of your guests have had enough to drink." Bea laughed, her eyes going from Chara to Quentin and back again.

Chara had to laugh at the bawdy words that Quentin sang in his melodic baritone, feeling his chest rise and fall against her back as he held her in front of him.

She found herself making coffee for the last hangerson, who all, with the exception of Grinnell, seemed to be old university cronies of Quentin's and Brad's.

Finally Bea pleaded that her hands were falling off and she couldn't play any longer. The men good-naturedly fell to discussing football teams, explaining to an interested Grinnell the intricacies of the megalomania known as American football.

Bea helped Chara clear away the coffee things, making a wry face at the heated discussion among the men.

"Football!" Bea exclaimed. "What they find so engrossing, I'll never know. Even when Brad and Q were playing, I found it hard to do anything more than pray they wouldn't be hurt."

"Quent played football?" Chara inquired, filling two

cups with coffee, then carrying them to the snack bar adjacent to the kitchen's work island.

"Chara, are you joking? Quent was a super quarterback. Brad always said he could have turned pro, but as you no doubt know, Quent was so bright, Phi Beta Kappa, the whole bit, that he had to turn his hand to something intellectually challenging—thus directing. Chara, why are you looking so surprised? Surely, you of all people must know what a catch you have." Bea rambled on, not noticing the flush deepening on Chara's cheeks. "I wish you could have seen how he had to beat them off with a stick, Chara. So many people think that Q is conceited. He isn't, as I'm sure you know, but he would have to be a fool not to realize his own charismatic appeal. He could as easily have been in front of the cameras as behind them." Bea nodded positively, then gave Chara a rueful grin. "There I go, running off at the mouth about one of my favorite people, but you have no idea what a good friend he's been to us. He's godfather to our sons, you know. What's this he tells me that you and he are going to be with Clem and her family for Christmas? How lucky for you. I just love Q's family and they must love you, Chara, because you're just perfect for Q," Bea said, leaning forward to clasp Chara's hand, and pausing to take a breath.

Chara smiled at Bea but sighed to herself as she realized that her time with Quentin was going to be very short. After tonight he would probably suggest that she see a lawyer soon. *Just the same,* she admonished herself, *you'll be with Clem and Jack over Christmas, so you'll have that to remember when Quentin is gone.*

At last the party was over, the Tilbys and Grinnell the last to go, with Bea insisting that they get together in January in Boston. Bea had already told Grinnell that he was coming to Boston with them for the holiday and that she wouldn't take no for an answer. Chara could tell that her photographer friend had fallen completely under Bea's spell and that he would enjoy his Christmas with the Tilbys.

When the door closed, Chara turned toward the kitchen.

"Where are you going, Chara?" Quentin snapped.

Without turning or stopping, she answered, "Kitchen." She knew he was following her even though the thick-piled carpeting muffled his footsteps. Grimly, when she stopped in front of the sink and started to rinse glasses to load in the dishwasher, he turned her toward him.

"We have to talk, Chara." His voice was low, but his tone was harsh.

"I think you did enough of that earlier this evening," Chara averred, freezing in his hold.

"Damn it, Chara. I won't have you kissing another man," Quentin rumbled.

"For your information, I wasn't kissing Ford. He was kissing me, as I told you, because I was under the mistletoe," Chara riposted.

"I don't care what the reason is. You are not to kiss another man. I noticed you didn't kiss your own husband at the party," Quentin lashed.

"We were never under the mistletoe together." Chara shrugged, pretending an indifference she didn't feel.

Before she could protest, Quentin had gripped her arm and dragged her down the short hallway to the foyer. Then he whirled her around to face him, still keeping hold of her two arms.

"Well, now we're under the mistletoe. So kiss your husband, Chara," Quentin said, never taking his eyes from Chara's face.

Feeling the red steal up her skin, Chara stood on tiptoe. Quentin released her arms to put his hands at her waist, drawing her closer. Chara pressed both hands to his chest, but still she couldn't reach his mouth.

"Pull my head down, Chara," Quentin whispered, urg-

186

ing her with little nods as her hands crept up his chest and around his neck. A thrill trembled through her as her slender fingers threaded the crisp curls at his neck. His head came down to her at the insistence of her fingers. Her tongue wet suddenly dry lips. When Quentin saw this, he covered them with his own, his mouth keeping hers parted. The kiss deepened. Chara had a floating feeling when she realized that Quentin had lifted her into his arms without lifting his mouth from hers.

Chara knew she should stop him—that he was only playing with her—but it felt so good to be held by him. For long moments she could convince herself that he cherished her, but she knew that in the cold light of day she would be humiliated if she didn't stop him from making love to her.

"Darling." Quentin breathed harshly, his voice unsteady as he headed toward her room. "I want you, little bride, but I think you know that." He laughed as he set her down on the bed.

When he straightened to pull at his tie and unbutton his shirt, Chara leaned up on one elbow. "No, Quent, I'm not going to sleep with you. Get out of my room."

"You little bitch," Quentin ground out.

For a moment Chara was sure he was going to follow her to bed.

Then, with an oath, he tore out of the room. The slamming of the door reverberated through the house. Then she heard the muffled slam of the outer door.

She turned her face into her pillow, harsh sobs tearing at her throat.

CHAPTER TEN

They had to circle the field twice before landing at Syracuse; thickly falling snow created problems for the snowplows on the landing field.

Chara gave a sigh of relief as the plane taxied to the deplaning point.

"Were you frightened, Chara?" Quentin asked, taking one of her clenched hands in both of his. His smile was reassuring and free of the cynical twist that was so often there.

"A little. I'm glad to be on the ground. I hope we'll be able to get home in this storm." Chara looked anxiously through the large glass doors that would take them to the car.

"Not to worry, wife." Quentin finally answered her after he had stored the luggage in the trunk and headed the car toward the thruway. "Despite the amount of snow, this is not a bad storm for New York State." Quentin laughed at her gasp. "There's no wind, Chara. Well, not a real blow that would drift the snow. The plows will be able to keep ahead of this. Be more sorry for the Tilbys and Grinnell. According to the weather reports, a big storm is heading toward Boston."

Chara watched Quentin's assured movements in guiding the car onto the thruway. Then, when she saw that he was quite at his ease, she decided to ask him something that had been bothering her for a long time.

"Quent?"

"Umm?"

"How is it that you have college friends on both sides of the Atlantic? Bea said you were a Phi Beta Kappa, but she didn't say why you went to school here and England," Chara asked, turning sideways on the seat so that she could look at him.

"Bea talks too much. All right, all right, don't look like that. I'll tell you. When I graduated from Harvard, I managed to wangle a fellowship to Oxford. That's where I met Ford Talbot. I was the one who brought him into the Exotica branch of Wainwright's." Quentin's lips tightened, as though he were remembering something distasteful. "Ironic, isn't it, that I should be the one to bring a man into the firm who falls in love with my wife," Quentin grated.

"I wish you wouldn't harp on that so," Chara said, confused by Quentin's mounting anger. "I enjoyed his company a few times. That's all."

"That's all, Chara?" Quentin exhaled through his mouth. "When I saw the two of you—"

"Quent, stop it. I explained that," Chara said.

"I'm not leaving him a clear field, Chara," Quentin said, as though Chara hadn't spoken. "From now on you and I are going to be together. New rules. We are going to seem like the happiest couple anywhere, Chara. When you wish to go somewhere, I'll take you."

"I don't understand you." Chara gulped, more relieved than she could ever tell him that he had no immediate plans to divorce her.

You have no pride, Chara Wainwright, she told herself. As scathing as she was to herself, no feeling was stronger than the relief she felt that she could remain with him for the time being.

Even with Quentin's constant assurances that the weather wasn't bad, Chara could see what a strain it was for him to drive down the lake road after the crawling, sometimes skidding progress they had made on the thruway. Several times Chara pressed her lips tight together to keep from screaming as the heavy car fishtailed close to the edge of the road.

"Those gullies are deep, aren't they, Quent?" Chara quavered after one hairy manuever that tested all Quentin's driving ability and made his well-muscled arms bulge with tension.

"Very. Don't worry, Chara. We only have a few miles to go. It did get worse than I thought it would. Do you think you'll mind being stranded with your husband?" Quentin didn't take his eyes off the road; one hand rubbed his eyelids.

"You're so tired, Quent. Let me drive the last miles," she pleaded, watching as he flexed his jaw.

"No. It's better not to stop in this stuff. We could have trouble getting traction again." Quentin shook his head. "You didn't answer my question, Chara. Do you think you'll mind being stranded with me for a few days?"

"Oh, I'll just rough it out, I guess," Chara answered airily. *I'll love it, you damn fool,* Chara wanted to scream at him. *I hope we're snowed in until spring.*

"Witch," Quentin growled, his laughter harsh. "I'll get you for that, Chara."

Chara laughed, feeling happy and free. *I'm going to have Quent all to myself,* she thought. *Tomorrow is Christmas and I'll have Quent under my Christmas tree.* It irked yet thrilled her that she felt like a schoolgirl again.

Chara's groan made Quentin stiffen, though he didn't take his eyes from the road.

"What's wrong, Chara?"

"We won't have a tree for tonight or tomorrow." Chara moaned, thinking of her stately balsam in the apartment in New York.

"Is that all?" Quentin grimaced. "Well, let me think. Yes, I think there are some evergreens near the cliff. After we have something to eat and rest, we'll take a look."

"Do you think there are any balsams?" Chara asked him, heaving a sigh of relief as they turned down the private road that led to their driveway.

"That I don't know, Chara. I'll call Jack and ask him. He and my father put in many of the trees on the property." Quentin gave a soft whistle as he stopped the car and activated the automatic garage door opener. The car skidded, then they were in the dry, dark interior.

Quentin put his head back on the seat rest and gave a prodigious yawn. "Pardon me, wife, but I'm tired." He turned to look at her. The soft smile he gave her made her heart flop like a fish in a creel.

While Chara went around pulling the drapes open to let in the pale afternoon light, she could hear Quentin conversing on the phone.

By the time he returned to her in the kitchen, she was slicing fresh-baked bread that had been under a cloth on the counter and putting thick slices of ham and cheese on it. She had found jars in the refrigerator marked HOME-MADE SOUP and ladled some into a pan.

Before she could set two places at the snack bar in the kitchen, Quentin had grabbed one of the sandwiches and was biting into it hungrily. He gave her a wolfish grin, his mouth packed full, when she scolded him about not waiting.

"Umm, that was good. I'm starving. I'll make the coffee, little bride," Quentin said, smacking his lips. When he passed her, carrying the coffee maker, she was stirring the soup. She felt his hand pat her behind. "Don't look so irritated, Chara." He mocked her gently. "It's very normal for a husband to pat his wife's derrière, especially if it's as cute as yours," he growled, then laughed at her as her neck reddened. "Sometimes you're so girlish, love, that I really do feel I'm married to a child and not a woman, except that when I stroke your lovely body, I know you're a woman or when you make those little snarling sounds in your throat."

"Quent, stop it." She swallowed hard. "You forgot the napkins." Chara didn't turn around. She was afraid he would see the glow she knew was in her eyes. *How wonderful it would be if Quent was like this all the time,* Chara dreamed, the wooden spoon in her hand stilling its circular motion. How right it felt to have him touch her.

They ate their lunch in companionable silence interspersed only with comments about the Christmas tree they hoped to cut on the property. "I talked to Jack and he said he isn't sure there are any balsams on the bank, but he knew there were some nice blue spruce that were good size for cutting. Would you settle for a substitute, Chara. Just this year? Next year, for sure, we'll have balsam for each place. I like the smell of them myself." Quentin gave her that lopsided grin that made her heart shift into high gear.

"I don't mind a blue spruce, Quent, as long as we have our own tree." Chara smiled at him, feeling shy all at once.

"Good. We'll have a beautiful tree." Quentin passed his cup to her to be refilled. "By the way, I told Jack we would pick up Gulliver and Cat when we came down for the Christmas buffet Clem always has on Christmas Eve. They usually go to evening service first. Would you like to accompany them, Chara?" Quentin asked.

"Yes, yes, I think I would like that. I used to attend service when I was at school in Rochester, but somehow

193

we never went much as a family." She shrugged, knowing she was babbling a little but was unable to stop the flow of remembrances. "Ken and I used to go sometimes, but then when he reached a certain age he didn't want to go anymore, and, well, I guess I didn't really like going by myself on Christmas Eve. There were always so many . . . families. Everyone seemed to belong to someone," she finished, not looking at Quentin.

"Yes, I know," Quentin said brusquely. "I remember when we used to go as a family when Amy and Dennis were babies. Jack would always try to make me go with him to the crying room if one of them acted up. He knew damn well that my mother would glare at me if I tried to refuse him. No matter how many times I told him that I wasn't taking Amy to the crying room one more time, he would still lean over my mother and ask me in a stage whisper to go with him. My mother would always announce that, of course, I would be glad to go."

"Where was Clem all this time?" Chara laughed, grateful that Quentin was distracting her from some painful memories of her own.

"Clem? You don't know Clem if you think she would ever spoil her Christmas outfit by holding messy children with ground-up graham crackers in their fists. No, sir, not our Clem," Quentin said, slandering his sister.

"Oh, I know you're wrong, Quent." Chara laughed. "Clem is the best of mothers and you know it." She hesitated. "Will you be going to service with us?"

"Only if you don't have graham crackers clutched in your fists." Quentin answered, ducking as Chara threw her napkin at him. He looked at her, his voice soft and amused. "Yes, I'm coming with you. Didn't you hear me when I said I wasn't going to let you out of my sight, wife? I meant it. Now, Chara, if you don't mind I'm going to have a nap. Join me?" Quentin leered, his eyes amused as he watched the color rise in her face.

"No, I . . . I don't think so. I'm going to clean up these things. You go ahead, Quent." Chara breathed hard, not looking at Quentin when he laughed and chucked her under the chin.

Chara stacked the dishes at the side of the sink, glad to have something to do with her hands when he departed, rather than face the turmoil in her mind. She wondered how long she could hold on to her sanity, trying to hide her true feelings from him. She scourged herself mentally for the traitorous body that wanted to follow after Quentin and climb into bed with him. "You are a first-class fool, Chara Wainwright," she muttered to herself, swiping a glob of dishwashing liquid from her cheek as she washed the bone china cups by hand. Despite Quentin's assurances that everything could be thrown into the dishwasher, it horrified her to think of putting the delicate china that had belonged to his grandmother in the appliance. When she told Quentin, he laughed and told her she was silly, but if it made her feel better, to do whatever she wished. After all, he assured her, all the plates, dishes, cutlery—everything belonged to her now. He told her that he had put the house on the bluff in her name and also the apartment in New York. When Chara would have protested and told Quentin how embarrassed she was, he overrode her by simply beginning to make love to her.

Chara sighed and wiped around the counter, then straightened up the large living room.

She knew that she wouldn't be able to nap, knowing that Quentin was in the next room, so she decided to have a bath. She ran water into the outsize round tub and started the Jacuzzi. She would bubble her disturbing thoughts away. She twisted her hair into a coil atop her head and pinned it tight, then lowered herself into the water, letting her body follow the soothing rhythm of the water. She lay there, dozing, not even caring to move, she felt so relaxed and calmed by the warmth and the motion of the water.

"Would you mind if I joined you?" Quentin asked, his smile lopsided.

"Not at all," Chara replied, her voice cool in spite of the tempest inside her. She felt her pulse was keeping time with the bubbling water. She felt utterly abandoned, knowing she wouldn't be able to keep him but wanting to store up memories of him she would treasure when she was alone. "Check to see if there's another bath sheet on the rack. If there isn't one there, you'll have to get one from the linen closet."

"I beg your pardon," Quentin rasped. "Repeat that."

Chara sighed, trying to keep her face bland, when the look in Quentin's eyes made fire leap through her veins. She felt too hot now. "I said, check and see if there is another bath—"

"I don't mean that, and you know it, Chara. Did you invite me into this tub with you?" he grated, fists clenched to his sides, white indentations bracketing his mouth.

"No, I did not invite you into this tub." Chara inhaled a breath, her voice still smooth. "I said I wouldn't mind if you joined me. I don't. Come on in." Chara took another deep breath, the feeling of power quite heady as she watched Quentin's narrow-eyed uncertainty. For the first time in their relationship, he wasn't sure of his footing, Chara thought, wanting to rub her hands together in glee.

"How many times have you bathed with someone, Chara?" Quentin barked, adopting the pugilist stance he always did when he was furious.

"Several." She giggled, the giddiness making her feel reckless. "I really can't remember how many." Chara shrugged, remembering exactly how many times Quentin had shampooed her hair in the lake, how many times he had gotten into the shower with her, how many times he had taken a bath with her. She felt like shouting at him to stop talking and get in the tub, but she didn't. She watched him through narrowed eyes, loving the hard, planed face that was white with tension and strain, caused, Chara hoped, by his intense desire to join her.

With a growl he stepped closer to her. "You little bitch," he snarled in a thickened voice, his hands reaching down, clawlike, to grasp her and almost lift her free of the tub. He shook her as though she were a Raggedy Ann doll. "Who was it? Talbot? Was it? Damn you, Chara, I won't allow it. Tell me who it was."

Chara watched him open-mouthed, her mind a blank, her eyes incredulous.

"Tell me, Chara. Has he had you? Did you sleep with him?" Quentin grated, his hands tightening on her shoulders.

"No, I've never slept with him." Rallying, she lashed back. "Damn you, Quent, let me go. Don't you manhandle me. You're out of line, Quent." Chara struggled. "It wasn't like that."

"He loves you, Chara. Yes, he loves you. He wanted to kill me the night of the party." He held her tighter when she shook her head no. "Yes, he wanted to kill me, and I know that because I wanted to kill him. I wanted nothing more than to beat him to a pulp," he shot out, his mouth working hard, a gray tinge to his face. A lock of his hair had fallen forward on his forehead, and it seemed to quiver in anger like the rest of him.

"You're mistaken, Quent." Chara shook her head. "It wasn't like that. I explained."

"Yes, you explained, but I know Talbot. He wants you, and he isn't going to get you, Chara. Damn it, no one is. Unless you want to see a bloody brawl between us, you'd do well to remember that. Stay away from him."

"Stop it," Chara hissed at him, her own anger rising, wriggling her shoulders in a vain effort to be free. "Stop talking like a barbarian. I won't stand for your acting this way. I won't let you be my keeper." Chara gulped, wanting to hit him.

His eyes ran down her naked form, a strange flicker in them as he studied her. "You're shivering." He lowered her back into the water and turned and left her without another word.

Chara had no idea how long she stayed where he had put her, but even when she dried herself, she couldn't stop shivering. Finally she switched on the heat lamp in the ceiling and warmed herself so that the shudders stopped racking her body. She dressed hurriedly.

Christmas Eve, Chara thought, *and Quent and I will not be speaking the entire time.* Her throat was tight with unshed tears as she wandered out into the main room and looked through the sliding glass doors to the patio, now filled with snow. She could almost hear Quentin's laughter as he barbecued their steaks last summer. Lord, it was going to be so hard to lose him.

At first the ring of the telephone behind her didn't penetrate her cloudy thoughts. She blinked and sighed, then picked up the phone.

"Chara? Chara, is that you?" Ken's voice sounded as though he were calling from the bottom of a well. "Chara, I won't be able to make it for Christmas. The landing fields are snowed in. Chara?"

"Yes, yes, Ken, I hear you." Chara swallowed hard, feeling doubly lost now that she wouldn't even have her brother with her. "I knew it was getting bad out there. Quent and I had a rough time traveling from Syracuse. Do you think you might be able to make it sometime during Christmas week?"

"I don't know. I'm hoping. I told the airlines that I wanted a reservation out as soon as they could manage it."

"I hate to think of your being alone." Chara tried to speak past a tear-clogged throat.

"Don't worry, sister mine, I'm having dinner with a

friend and his family. I'll get there, don't worry." Ken's voice changed. "Chara, is something wrong? You sound sad."

"No, nothing is wrong, Ken, except that I'm going to miss having you with me," Chara said, forcing her voice to sound lighter.

"Are you sure, Chara? I want so badly for you to be happy. You've done so much for me."

"I'm happy, Ken. I'll look forward to seeing you for New Year's. Bye now. Merry Christmas."

Chara replaced the receiver and stared out the window again. She jumped when she heard the slam of the outer door. Then there was a rapid clicking sound on the tile floor before Gulliver's head came into view from the hall. He spotted her at the same time she saw him and launched his body across the room, whining his eagerness to reach her. "Darling Gulliver, where did you come from? You're all snow. You look so beautiful. I've missed you." Chara burst into tears with her face pressed into his cold, wet coat.

"As I've said before, I wish I could get one-half that response from you." Quentin spoke, his voice flat. Then he gave her a twisted smile. "Dry your tears, Chara. I've brought you an early Christmas present." From his coat Quentin extracted a snow-white cat, not quite a kitten but not a full-grown cat either.

Rising from Gulliver's side, one hand swiping at the tears on her cheeks, she reached out to take the furry ball and clasp it to her, rubbing her cheek on the fluffy white fur. Gulliver sniffed his approval at her side. Chara laughed when the kitten reached down and cuffed the panting dog on the nose.

"They're great friends. They sleep together and are almost inseparable, Amy says. By the way, Amy and Clem send their best and say they can't wait to see you this evening."

Chara risked a glance at Quentin's bland features, wondering at this change in him. Not two hours ago he had been raging at her. Chara mentally shrugged, hoping they could have a truce through Christmas.

"Now close your eyes, Chara, I have something else for you," Quentin insisted.

Chara listened to the rustling noises, then an odor assailed her nostrils. Her eyes flew open.

"A balsam! Quent, where did you get it? It's beautiful. Put it right there. No. Put it over there. No. Wait a minute. Let me think." Chara mused, putting her index finger between her teeth as she slowly turned around.

"Damn it, Chara, this may not be as big as the one in New York, but I still don't feel like holding it forever."

"All right, all right. Put it in front of the sliding glass doors. Oh, Quent, do we have a holder?" Chara wailed, wanting to get the tree up right away.

"Don't worry, I have everything. I borrowed Dennis's snowmobile to bring the things. Gulliver ran alongside like a good boy."

"Of course. He's such a gentleman," Chara purred, scratching the ecstatic dog under the chin.

The tree was decorated in a haphazard but laughing fashion. Only three of the bulbs were duds, but the ornaments Quentin had scrounged up from Clem's house were numerous and varied. Chara watched as Quentin lifted a rather battered cloth Santa from a box and studied it, a pensive smile on his face. He turned to look at her, his smile widening as he handed it to her.

"Clem and I helped our mother make several of these. I thought at the time they must be the most beautiful ornaments in the world." Quentin's smile was cynical, but his eyes were warm.

"He still is quite beautiful," Chara said, taking the Santa from Quentin and stroking it, able quite easily to picture Quentin the boy eagerly helping his mother.

"Look at him, Gully darling." Chara, sitting cross-legged on the carpet in front of the tree showed it to the tail-wagging dog, who promptly took it into his mouth and walked around them, head high.

"Chara, for God's sake, don't encourage him. He's rocking the tree with that damn tail of his." Quentin laughed, shooting out an arm to steady the evergreen.

The closeness between them persisted, so that by the time Chara came out of her bath before getting dressed to go to Clem's, she was bubbling with Christmas spirit. She took the small gift wrapped in silver paper that she had purchased in New York for Quentin and put it under the tree. Then she stood there in her silky wrap, switched on the tree lights, and stared at the tree without moving. No matter how angry Quentin became with her, it wouldn't change the fact that this would be the happiest holiday she had ever spent or would ever spend because she was with him. She gave a deep sigh, hugging herself.

"What are you thinking, Chara? Why the big sigh?" Quentin asked just behind her, making her jump. Before she could turn, he had slipped his arms around her and rested his cheek on her hair.

"I . . . I was just looking at our tree and thinking about Christmas," Chara whispered, her heart beating so wildly in her she was sure he could hear it. She felt him stiffen, then look over her shoulder.

"What's that under the tree?" he asked, then, turning her in his arms, he let one thumb rub her cheek. "Are we putting our gifts under the tree now?" Quentin asked, his eyes roving over her face. "Good." He answered himself, not waiting for her reply. "I'll get mine." He dropped a light kiss on her nose and sprinted for his room whistling "God Rest Ye Merry Gentlemen."

He was back in an instant, not quite meeting her gaze as he placed a small jeweler's box and a larger clothing box under the tree. "Let's open them now, Chara," he urged, his grin boyish.

Chara nodded, feeling her skin glow under Quentin's look. "You first, Quent."

"No, ladies first. Here, Chara, open this first." Quentin pressed the small box wrapped in gold foil into her hand. They both sank down on the rug in front of the tree as Chara carefully unwrapped and displayed the delicate bracelet in gold filigree with two short words scrolled in sapphires.

"It says something, but I can't read it, Quent. What does it say?" Chara asked, staring at the lovely thing as she turned it in her hands.

"It's German script, very hard to read. Here, look at your other gift," Quentin persisted as he started to tear the elaborate striped bow from the paper before Chara with a yelp took it from him and carefully removed the wrappings to lift the gossamer-sheer silk nightie from the box. "It's the same blue as your eyes," Quentin said, his smile lopsided as he watched her blush.

"Thank you. I love my presents," Chara whispered as Quentin murmured, "Then thank me properly," and leaned closer. She took a deep breath and placed her mouth on his. Then Quentin took over, folding her to him, then pressing her backward to the floor while still kissing her. When his mouth left hers to place feather-light kisses on her throat, then edged down farther, Chara could feel her control slipping. She mustn't let him ever find out how much she loved him. "Quent, Quent, you haven't opened your gift."

For a moment she thought he wasn't going to stop, then he inhaled and lifted his head. "Coward," he muttered before rolling away from her and picking up the elongated jeweler's box. "Well, I know it's not a shirt and the box is too short to be a tie . . ."

"Open it, open it." Chara clasped her hands in front of

her, feeling a beading of moisture on her upper lip. When Quentin opened the leather case and picked up the tiny silver sculpture, Chara held her breath. The silence was interminable as Quentin gazed at the miniature sailboat and two people with the letter Q inscribed on the top of the sail and the letter C on the bottom. "Do you like it?" Chara burst out at his continued silence.

Quentin looked up at her as she scrambled to her knees, his hot, silver eyes flowing over her, his hard mouth softening to a smile that made her heart knock. "I've never had anything I liked better. It's perfect, Chara. Come here."

Chara looked at him and knew she would give herself away if he touched her, then he would know that she loved him. She saw herself pleading with him not to leave her and recoiled. The action brought her to her feet. She could feel Quentin's puzzled stare as she looked around the room. "We have to hurry now, Quent. Clem will be waiting." As Chara rushed from the room clutching her presents she heard him snarl, "Let her wait."

It was a beautiful Christmas Eve—the church service, the party afterward at Clem's house. She met many of their friends and some of Dennis's and Amy's that she had met before. The best part for Chara had been when they had all exchanged gifts before going to church. Chara felt she was family. She strolled out into the solarium that was cooler than the rest of the house, relying on its heat from the solar catchers that Jack had installed. A huge spruce was in the center of the room, its tiny lights the only illumination. A few couples were dancing, but she didn't notice Quentin and Letty Armor until she turned to leave the room. "She's been crazy about Quent for years," Chara could hear Amy telling her when the woman had come up to Quentin earlier in the evening and claimed him for a dance. Jealously forked through Chara as she watched the woman reach up and touch Quentin's mouth. Chara couldn't stop staring. Almost as though he could feel her look, Quentin lifted his head and gazed at her. Then he turned and leaned down to press his mouth on Letty Armor's eager one.

Gasping with rage and pain, Chara turned away, stumbling around some dancers who were swaying to a throbbing beat. She mumbled an apology, then wended her way to the living room where she found Clem. Chara knew that Clem had an anxious look when Chara excused herself, but she didn't explain. She couldn't.

When Dennis offered to take her up the hill on his snowmobile, Chara accepted, wondering in a detached way if people ever did die of a broken heart. She hardly felt the cold wind blowing against her face as they climbed the hill.

"Are you all right, Chara? Do you want me to come in with you?" Dennis asked, trying to fend off the ecstatic Gulliver who met them at the door.

"Why don't you come in and I'll make you a cup of coffee before you tackle the hill again?" Chara tried to smile. Fussing with the coffee things allowed her time to get her churning stomach back to a semblance of normalcy. She still had the feeling she wanted to smash things, but Dennis's easy banter calmed her, so she could face him with a real smile.

Dennis's anecdotes about Gulliver and Cat made her smile at first but his descriptions and antics as he imitated the animals made her laugh. She could feel much of her tension dissipating under the persuasive charm of Quentin's nephew. After a graphic account of Cat's predilection for Jack's morning cereal, Chara was gasping.

"Your girl friend must love you if you keep her entertained like this all the time." Chara wiped her eyes.

"I don't have a special girl. I'm waiting until I find someone like you, Chara. Quent's lucky. I wish I'd seen you first," Dennis said, leaning across the table to cover Chara's limp hand with his.

With a blast of cold air from the garage Quent appeared, his derisive smile marking the progress of Dennis's hand as he removed it from Chara's.

"If you've finished your coffee, you'd better get back down there, Dennis. You may have to take some of the guests home." Quentin clipped his words in Dennis's direction, but he kept his gaze on Chara.

Dennis's mumbled good night and Merry Christmas weren't even answered by Quentin. He stood full in the doorway so Chara couldn't see Dennis to the door.

The silence lengthened between them even as they heard the roaring sound of the snowmobile fading down the hill.

Chara rinsed the cups at the sink, then attempted to leave the kitchen.

"Where the hell do you think you're going, Chara?" Quentin snarled.

"To bed. Where else would I be going at one o'clock in the morning?" she snapped, then tried to push past him, but Quentin caught at her, turning her in his arms, pressing his hard, angry mouth on hers. The kiss lengthened and deepened. Chara could feel herself breaking apart as his mouth moved over hers.

When he finally lifted his head, she put one hand to her trembling mouth. Chara tried to wrench free, but Quentin's steellike arms held her fast.

"Let me go." Chara tried to swallow the bitterness that clogged her throat. "Haven't you enough butterflies pinned to your board? So let me tell you that this butterfly is escaping," Chara rasped. "No more of your Marat–Sade games for me. I don't like being punished, being hated."

"Hated? Damn you, Chara, I love you," Quentin grated, a pallor fading his dark skin, his hands dropping to his sides.

205

"No," she said. "You don't love me." Her mouth shook.

"Yes, damn you, I do," Quentin thrust at her, a violence in him that she had seen when Ford Talbot had kissed her under the mistletoe. "What were you doing with that nephew of mine? I'll break his damn neck for him."

Chara stood frozen, staring up at him, her hands and feet beginning to tingle as though she were coming to life. Pins of feeling tore through her as blood started to pump through her. Could she believe him? Chara swallowed loudly, her stomach knotting and unknotting, her eyes eating up Quentin as though she couldn't have enough of him.

"From the beginning, Chara, I've loved you," Quentin muttered, his one hand going out to touch her cheek, then pulling back. "Do you remember the day we first met?"

"Yes, you despised me. Propositioning me the moment you took hold of my hand, then verbally repeating the same invitation." Chara mumbled, not taking her eyes from that hard mouth, the flaring silver eyes, the high-planed face with the straight black brows, the strong nose, the rocklike chin.

"No." Quentin glowered, his hands clenching at his sides. "I just knew I wanted you more than I had ever wanted a woman. I knew that I didn't want any other man touching you, yet I never guessed you would be untouched."

"You hated my being a virgin. You hated marrying me. I could see your contempt every time you looked at me. You felt trapped," Chara accused.

"No," Quentin said in a low voice. "What you saw was fear. I rushed you into marriage because that was the only way I could think to hold you. I was sure you despised me for treating you the way I had. I assumed you were experienced and made love to you as if you were. God, Chara, I nearly went into shock when I discovered I was

206

the first. It made me so happy. I knew I couldn't let you go," Quent said. "I didn't even know I was in love with you then. I just knew I couldn't let you escape me. The longer we were together the worse I became. I couldn't let you out of my sight. When you left me and went to England, I wanted to go after you and drag you back. Then I was afraid."

He turned away from her, pacing to the fireplace and placing one foot on the raised hearth. A not too steady hand pushed through his thick hair. "At first I thought I would give you time. Whatever was bothering you would disappear, I thought. You might come to miss me, because I was missing you like hell. I went back to California, buried myself in my work, but your face was always there. Ask anybody, I was a bear to work with. I drove them all like I drove myself. Most of them thought I was going crazy. They were right. I took some women out, figuring I'd get over you the same way I could get over any woman —with another woman. It didn't work. Nothing worked. I saw you everywhere."

Quentin took a deep breath, leaned one shoulder against the stone mantel and turned to watch Chara. "There's no one but you. There can never be, no matter what you decide. God knows I wanted to break the hold you have on me." He gave a mirthless laugh. "For the first time in my life I couldn't work up any enthusiasm for something that I used to consider second nature. I knew I was pretty far gone when I took out someone like Gypsy Cane and couldn't wait to leave her at the door." Quentin gave a twisted smile. "And it wasn't that she wasn't willing either."

"I'm sure of that," Chara snapped, wanting to tear at him as the hot jealousy burned her. "What about Letty Armor? And Zina Prentiss? That looked pretty enthusiastic. You kissed them. You knew that I saw you do it." She flared up, angry anew at the thought of him with the other women.

"Were you jealous?" Quentin whispered, his narrow-eyed stare probing her.

"Why should I be jealous of such a common occurrence?" Chara snapped waspishly, the old defenses erecting themselves at once. "You forget, Quent, that my mother was only too happy to inform me about the bedroom athlete I had married," Chara said, swallowing hard.

Quentin looked away, staring at the modern painting of yellow and orange slashes that hung over the fireplace. "Damn it, Chara, I don't deny there were women, that they were a big part of my life—until I met you." He turned, growling. "Do you want me to sign an affidavit? You're the only woman in my life." He stared at her.

Chara recalled that dreadful trip to England and why she had rushed from him as though all the demons of Hades pursued her. "You hated it, having to deal with both of us. I couldn't take that," Chara whispered, not seeing his arrested look, trying to swallow the painful lump of memory clogging her throat. "I picked up the extension and heard you talking to Judson, talking about taking care of my mother and . . . and me." Chara choked, jumping to her feet and facing away from Quentin. She walked toward the stereo, hating the charged silence, wondering what he was thinking.

"My God, Chara," Quentin said hoarsely. "I'm not involved with your mother in any way except business. She's a good satiric writer. That's all she's ever been." He paused, taking a deep breath. "I'm not saying your mother wouldn't have welcomed a different relationship with me. I knew she would have, but she does not interest me that way. I don't even like her much and avoided most social contact with her. That day I met you, well, I was there because I wanted her to make some changes on a script of hers. The best thing about that day was meeting you. I have never lied to you, Chara." Quentin watched her.

"My mother said that I could never hold your interest, but you certainly seemed . . . to care when Ford Talbot—" Chara began.

"He was pawing you!" Quentin snarled, his jaw working hard. "I wanted to kill him. I wanted to shut you up in a room with me forever. Do you know how many times I've wanted to kick myself around the block for mooning over you like a lovesick teen-ager?" he groaned.

"You don't do that." Chara laughed, wanting to be closer to him.

"Yes, I do. I can't help it," he averred, his eyes going over her. "You were a baby compared to me, even if you were a very poised career woman. Oh, I knew I could make you respond to me, arouse you." He laughed gently when she reddened. "But I wanted more, Chara. I wanted all of you—your thoughts, your feelings, your present, your future. A thousand years wouldn't be long enough to live with you, Chara." He clenched his fists. "I hung around you like a schoolboy waiting for you to smile at me. I made a damn fool of myself. I hated it."

Proud Quentin Wainwright making such an admission brought Chara's mouth agape. "Is that why you glowered at me all the time. I thought it was because you hated me, that you felt trapped," Chara whispered, the singing in her veins getting stronger. She looked at an African violet on a nearby table, mesmerized by its royal velvet hue, wondering why she had thought that she didn't like African violets before now.

"Damn it, Chara. Haven't you been listening to me? I love you. I've been trying to make you love me. I tried to keep it casual at first—"

"Casual?" Chara murmured, trying to still the quiver of laughter on her lips. "Every time I turned around you were making love to me. I would hardly call that keeping it casual."

"I couldn't keep my hands to myself," he snarled. "I kept having to touch you, kiss you, make love to you. Damn you, Chara. You've had me on a string since we met. That's why I had to lash out at you. Do you understand what I'm saying?" He made a swift circuit of the room, then stopped in front of her, legs apart, arms akimbo. "I was a panting idiot. You sank my boat without a fight." He grasped her shoulder. "You didn't have a percentage point of sophistication or artifice compared to the women I had been used to and I had handled them easily. Then you came into my life and I didn't do one thing right."

Chara stared at him. It gave her satisfaction to know that he had suffered as much as she had. She gave a rueful smile when she saw him grind his teeth in angry frustration. How many times she had done just that when she had thought of him with other women!

"Darling, what are you thinking?" Quentin asked, his voice thick.

"How strange it is that so many times our thoughts paralleled each other's, yet we tried never to show what we were thinking. How awful to think that our lives were separating and—"

"No," Quentin snarled. "I had no intention of letting you go. I was coming to London with or without the play. It was I who arranged for you and Grinnell to be sent to New York by Exotica so that you would be out of Talbot's reach, but the bastard followed you. I wanted to kill him," he growled, then he leaned over Chara, letting his tongue trace her cheek. "I was also ready to beg you not to go with him."

"Beg? You?" Chara scoffed, but her voice was light as joy coursed through her. "On bended-knee perhaps?" Chara burbled, her hand idly switching on the stereo.

210

"Yes," he ground out behind her, "if that's what it takes. You won't divorce me easily, Chara. I'll fight you every step of the way."

Chara took a deep, relieved breath. She wouldn't have to leave him. They would be together. She remembered little Robin in England who wanted "Aunt Cawa" to have a baby so that he could play with him. Gleefully she patted her tummy, thinking how Robin would be one of the first ones she would tell when she and Quentin were having a child. *God,* she thought, *how wonderful it is just to think about. Quent is mine! Now. When he's an old man, he'll be so distinguished, so . . .*

"What are you thinking now, love? You've drifted away again." Quentin said, his lips at her neck.

Chara whirled around just as the strains of a love song filled the room. "I never wanted the divorce. You did. My mother told me."

"Damn your mother," Quentin barked. "She has nothing to do with us." Quentin's voice trailed off as his attention was caught by the music. "Dance with me, Chara. I think of all love songs as ours," Quentin muttered, reaching for her and holding her tight against him.

Their steps were silent and they stumbled a bit on the carpet, but it felt so right to Chara to be held by Quentin. When he told her to sing to him, she did, the words throbbing as she threw her arms around his neck. *Quentin loved her.* The words spun in her head as she mouthed the words of the love song. "And with you I'm born again . . ."

They stood swaying together as the music ended. Chara felt bereft when Quentin leaned back from her a fraction.

"I love you, Chara."

"I never wanted the divorce, Quent," she said, pressing her face into his shoulder. "Well, maybe at first I did. You frightened me for a short time, then I don't know what happened. Sometimes we would seem so close and I wanted things to stay that way. Then at other times you would be so angry at me that I knew you hated me and considered my being with you an intolerable burden."

"I never felt that, not once," Quentin mumbled into her hair, his open hand stroking her back from neck to coccyx.

"What about the night I found Gulliver? You were furious with me." Chara gulped, threading her fingers through the short curly hair at his nape, delighted when she heard him gasp with pleasure.

"Not at *you*, Chara. Those damned boys called me your father. You are so young-looking. I didn't want to be reminded about how innocent you were even at the ripe old age of twenty-five."

"Twenty-six, now," Chara murmured, biting the edge of his chin, watching those silver eyes catch fire.

"Tell me how you feel, Chara. Once you told me you loved me. I lived on that, Chara. Do you still, even a little?" Quentin leaned over, flushing a little at her gaze. "See, that's how little pride I have where you're concerned. I want you, Chara. I want to take care of you."

Chara felt she would explode. She let her hands frame his face as she looked at him fully, not hiding the sheen of happiness in her eyes. "I have always wanted to tell you how much I enjoyed my wedding night. It was quite beautiful," she whispered, loving the feel of his smooth-shaven cheeks under her caressing fingers, smiling as his flush deepened at her words. "Of course you're not always so gentle and loving. You shocked poor Mark and Brian when you came into the garage that night. I'm sure they think you're a very violent man, Mr. Wainwright." Chara reached up and brushed his mouth with hers. Before she could draw back, Quentin had lifted her from the floor and kissed her hard.

"They're lucky they're alive. I won't let anyone near you, wife of mine," he said, an agate look to his eyes, as though his thoughts were most unpleasant.

Chara felt light as a bubble as she dangled in Quentin's arms. She was so close to him that she could see the pores of his face and the faint gray shadow of beard that was never quite shaved away. Of its own volition her one hand lifted to his face, one finger outlining the strong slash of his dark brow. It was as though she had to touch him, to mark him as her own.

"Enjoying yourself, darling?" Quentin asked, a thread of amusement in his voice.

"Yes," Chara answered, aware that he had read what she was thinking, knowing somehow that they would always know what the other was thinking because they were like two halves of a whole. "When I traveled through Spain with Wendy I learned a beautiful expression . . . about us."

"You did?" Quentin asked her, holding her easily, his eyes a hot silver on her face. "Are you going to tell it to me?"

"Do you speak Spanish, Quent?" Chara asked him, touching the corner of his mouth, watching the play of emotions on his face as she did this.

"Some. I've traveled in Mexico and made a movie down there once." He still spoke softly, but she saw his face darken a deep red.

"What is it, Quent? What are you thinking?" she whispered, leaning closer to him.

"Do you care for any of them, Chara? Talbot? Anyone else?" Quentin breathed thickly as he eased her back onto her feet. He didn't release her from his arms.

"Ford Talbot was just a friend to me, Quent. Nothing more than that." She sensed that she couldn't tell him that she allowed Ford to get close to her because she thought she had lost him and Ford helped her over a bad time. She did not think she could convince Quentin that Ford had restored her self-confidence—that he made her feel wanted. She knew that Quentin would be hurt by hearing that, no matter how hard she tried to convince him that Ford was more like a healer than a lover to her. Someday when their confidence in each other abounded, she might tell him, but not now.

"If there's no one else, then you can stay with me. I'll teach you to care for me, Chara. We'll go everywhere together. We'll travel, do so much together," Quentin urged, his eyes holding her, his hands tightening. "I'll make you happy, Chara, you'll see."

"Not if you're going to be kissing other women." Chara glared, her hands clenching into fists where they lay on his chest.

Hard laughter rumbled in his chest. "I'm asking you again, love. Were you jealous when I kissed Letty? I wanted you to be."

"I could have killed you," Chara confessed, her voice shaking as she thought of the other woman clinging to him.

"Good." Quentin kissed her hard, his mouth questing and possessive. "It's a start. I'll teach you to care for me. Someday you'll tell me again that you love me. I want to hear that, Chara. I need to."

Chara reached up to clasp his neck. The flash of the gold bracelet on her wrist caught her eye. "What does my bracelet say, Quent? You said it was German script. Do you know what it says?" Chara watched him, surprised to see a red flush on his cheeks again.

"Yes, I know what it says, my darling. It says *Ewig Dein* and it means Eternally Yours. Pretty sugary, I suppose you're thinking?" Quentin's derisive smile was for himself this time, Chara was sure.

She couldn't stop the flow of happiness through her. It tidal-waved inside her, spilling into every corner of her being. Her hands trembled as they feathered over his cheeks. "Do you think we might begin my lessons now?" Chara purred, pressing her hips closer to him in a sensual

214

rotation. She felt him stiffen for a moment, his breath hissing from his body in surprise.

"What lessons are we speaking of, Chara?" Quentin asked, his breath ragged as his hands dropped to her moving hips.

Chara let her eyes widen in mock surprise, her fingers teasing the crisp hair on his neck. "Why, Quent, have you forgotten? You were going to teach me to love you? I have a feeling that I'm going to be a very apt pupil. Any questions?" Chara bit him on the chin, loving the feeling of power when his heart started to race.

"Just once," he husked. "Tell me what the beautiful expression is that you learned in Spain. Remember? You said it was about us. Tell me what it is."

"The Spanish say that when you have found the right person for you, it's finding the other half of your orange. Isn't that like us? We fit, don't we, Quent?"

"Oh, God, yes, we fit. You are so much a part of me, there is no way to get you out of me."

"I hate to repeat myself, but are those lessons going to begin soon?"

His mouth dropped to hers, making hers bloom open. It was a kiss of possession and Chara reveled in the entire ravishment. Her heart throbbed against his as the heat built between them.

Without removing his mouth from hers, he swept her up into his arms. She kissed him, locking her arms around his neck, delighting in the knowledge that he wanted her as badly as she wanted him. He loved her, her heart sang inside her, the words zinging through her veins. He placed her on their bed and began to undress her, his hands trembling as his eyes roved over her slender body, naked to his gaze.

Chara cursed his shirt buttons as she undressed him, feeling restless and uninhibited.

"Don't talk like that, darling." Quentin laughed, his

body shuddering against her as she touched him with light caresses.

She pulled him down to her, muttering about stupid trousers and that damned belt. "I missed sleeping with you so much when I was in England. I used to wake up feeling lost. I didn't like the feeling."

"God, Chara, most nights I didn't sleep. I'd work or pace or both. It was hell without you. I couldn't go through another time like that."

The rough hair of his chest teased her breasts, making her gasp and wriggle closer to him.

"Chara, baby, slowly, slowly. I want it to be so beautiful for you," Quentin husked, his mouth trailing over her body, stilling her turning head as the fever rose in her.

"Quent, Quent, I love you. It's so beautiful for me now. I can't believe how you can make me feel," Chara sobbed, her hands clutching at his hair to bring his mouth to hers again. She moaned as they entered the eye of the hurricane, knowing that this storm had caused her to become more of a woman than she had ever been and now would never allow her to go back to what she was, even if she chose to do so, and she did not. She was Quentin's now for all time, and he would know it. She wanted him to know.

Then she was past thinking as she heard him groan out her name against her shoulder—the long, painful need of his destroying the last vestige of her control. She held nothing back. She was all his, sunk in a whirl of feeling that was beyond anything she had ever felt before with Quentin. It was as though their want of each other spiraled them to another planet of emotion.

Sleep came to them both, almost at once. They still lay wrapped in one another's arms.

Chara woke to the sound of scratching and the brightness of winter sunshine refracting from the snow. She

216

knew it was Gulliver when the scratching on the door became insistent. When she tried to ease away from Quentin, he mumbled something and took Chara closer to him. "Darling? Quent, just let me up for a moment. I want to let Gulliver outside." Chara laughed softly, her hands running up his hard body, happy that she was free to touch him whenever she wished.

"Tell me you love me first." Quentin nuzzled her sleepily, not loosening his hold.

"I love you, my beautiful husband. Merry Christmas."

"Men aren't beautiful, but you are." Quentin rolled over, imprisoning her under him. "But I love to hear you say things like that anyway. I won't let you go until you kiss me. I want my Christmas present now," Quentin insisted, rubbing his lips back and forth on hers.

"You *are* beautiful, other men aren't, but you are. And you've had your Christmas present. Don't you remember?"

"I mean my *real* Christmas present—you. That's my lifetime present that I'll want you to give me over and over again. I'll never get used to having you, Chara. It will always be mint-new for me."

Chara sighed, drinking in his words, feeling bubbleheaded, knowing she could scale Mt. Everest at that moment. She felt the heat begin to rise in her as Quentin's hand stroked her body. Wriggling with pleasure and anticipation, Chara closed her eyes, just as Gulliver gave a long, mournful howl. Her eyes flew open, alight with mirth, as Quentin gave an angry groan, then rolled onto his back.

"I wonder if that fool hound knows how close he's coming to being strangled."

"I'll be right back, Quent." Chara giggled, scrambling out of their bed, aware that Quentin's eyes were on her nude form as she reached for her wrap.

"Hurry back, lady love."

"Of course, man love."

Hurriedly she let Gulliver out through the door leading from the garage, shivering at the icy blast of air but appreciating the stark whiteness of the snow glistening in the sunshine. They would be able to cross-country ski on Christmas Day, Chara thought, and from now on all her plans would include Quentin. The thought made her heart thump. When she returned to the kitchen, Cat was waiting, looking at her with expectant eyes. Chara laughed as the purring feline contorted herself through Chara's legs, then when the bowl of dry cat food and bowl of milk were placed on the floor, Cat ignored Chara and turned to the food without a backward glance. "Lotus eater," Chara crooned, stroking the back of the contentedly munching cat.

On impulse Chara went into the sitting room and bent down under the Christmas tree to lift the blue nightgown Quentin had given her from its box. It felt like a silky nothing in her hands. Rushing through a warm shower, she donned the transparent gown, wide-eyed at the way it clung to her figure, delineating her breasts and hips. She touched Joy perfume to her pulse points and took a deep breath before going into their bedroom where Quentin was lying on his stomach, his face pushed into the pillow.

Some slight sound, or an instinct, made him lift up and look around in her direction. Then he whirled to a sitting position, his liquid, silver eyes melting her. "God, Chara, you're exquisite even if you are a mite too slim. Come here to me and explain why you ever went on a diet. That really made me angry," Quentin muttered, his hands pulling her down to him, his lips feathering her cheek, her ears, her hair.

"I never dieted, Quent. No, really, I didn't," Chara said as he raised his head from her shoulder to look at her. "After I left you and went to England, I found I couldn't eat. It made me sick to eat most of the time. I pined for you, Quent. I loved you so much and missed you so much that I just couldn't eat."

Quentin didn't let her continue, coming down to her with a groan. His mouth fastened to hers and like a flash fire, their desire for one another engulfed them.

"Love me, Quent," Chara cried, entwined with him, feeling the agonizing need for his exploding within her, knowing Quentin held back his needs while fanning hers to white hot. Chara felt dizzy and dry-mouthed as she clutched at him. "Quent, I love you. I love you . . ."

"And I love you, Chara," Quentin gasped. "Now, love, now."

Drained and relaxed, enfolded in his arms, Chara lifted one finger to trace his black brows. "Does everyone feel this way when they love each other, Quent?" she asked

"I don't know, but they should. It's so perfect with us."

"It's just like a new world for me. With you I'm born again. It's all the happiness I've ever known." Chara blushed. "Maybe we'll have a baby. I want a boy just like you."

"Do you, love?" Quentin laughed gently, his eyes still roving over her as though he would never have enough of looking at her. "Well, then, if that's what you want, we'll just have to work on it. Very hard, I think," Quentin said softly, his body moving down to hers.

Dell Bestsellers

☐ **NOBLE HOUSE** by James Clavell............$5.95 (16483-4)
☐ **PAPER MONEY** by Adam Smith...............$3.95 (16891-0)
☐ **CATHEDRAL** by Nelson De Mille..............$3.95 (11620-1)
☐ **YANKEE** by Dana Fuller Ross....................$3.50 (19841-0)
☐ **LOVE, DAD** by Evan Hunter.......................$3.95 (14998-3)
☐ **WILD WIND WESTWARD**
  by Vanessa Royal...$3.50 (19363-X)
☐ **A PERFECT STRANGER**
  by Danielle Steel..$3.50 (17221-7)
☐ **FEED YOUR KIDS RIGHT**
  by Lendon Smith, M.D. $3.50 (12706-8)
☐ **THE FOUNDING**
  by Cynthia Harrod-Eagles.........................$3.50 (12677-0)
☐ **GOODBYE, DARKNESS**
  by William Manchester...............................$3.95 (13110-3)
☐ **GENESIS** by W.A. Harbinson.....................$3.50 (12832-3)
☐ **FAULT LINES** by James Carroll................$3.50 (12436-0)
☐ **MORTAL FRIENDS** by James Carroll $3.95 (15790-0)
☐ **THE SOLID GOLD CIRCLE**
  by Sheila Schwartz......................................$3.50 (18156-9)
☐ **AMERICAN CAESAR**
  by William Manchester................................$4.50 (10424-6)

At your local bookstore or use this handy coupon for ordering:

Dell   **DELL BOOKS**
P.O. BOX 1000, PINE BROOK, N.J. 07058-1000

Please send me the books I have checked above. I am enclosing $_____ (please add 75c per copy to cover postage and handling). Send check or money order—no cash or C.O.D.'s. Please allow up to 8 weeks for shipment.

Mr./Mrs./Miss_____

Address_____

City_____State/Zip_____

The unforgettable saga of a magnificent family

IN JOY AND IN SORROW

by JOAN JOSEPH

They were the wealthiest Jewish family in Portugal, masters of Europe's largest shipping empire. Forced to flee the scourge of the Inquisition that reduced their proud heritage to ashes, they crossed the ocean in a perilous voyage. Led by a courageous, beautiful woman, they would defy fate to seize a forbidden dream of love.

A Dell Book $3.50   (14367-5)

The second volume in the spectacular Heiress series

The Cornish Heiress

by Roberta Gellis

bestselling author of
The English Heiress

Meg Devoran—by night the flame-haired smuggler, Red Meg. Hunted and lusted after by many, she was loved by one man alone...

Philip St. Eyre—his hunger for adventure led him on a desperate mission into the heart of Napoleon's France.

From midnight trysts in secret smugglers' caves to wild abandon in enemy lands, they pursued their entwined destinies to the end—seizing ecstasy, unforgettable adventure—and love.

A Dell Book   **$3.50**   **(11515-9)**